You have been chosen for your special skills to do something that urgently needs to be done. To learn more, come to the Ballroom at 3:30. Don't miss this. It will be worth your while - $$$

TWO WEEKS EARLIER . . .

SWINDLE

GORDON KORMAN

Scholastic Inc.

New York Toronto London Auckland Sydney
Mexico City New Delhi Hong Kong Buenos Aires

For Willie, G.F.

This book was originally published in hardcover
by Scholastic Press in 2008.

ISBN-13: 978-0-439-90345-5
ISBN-10: 0-439-90345-9

17 16   13 14/0

Printed in the U.S.A.   40
This edition first printing, April 2009

The text type was set in ITC Century.
Book design by Elizabeth B. Parisi and Marilyn Acosta

1

SNEAKING OUT AT NIGHT – HELPFUL HINTS:

(i) When lying to your parents, maintain EYE CONTACT.

(ii) Make sure you ask permission to attend the correct FAKE SLEEPOVER. (Boys – Stan Winter's place. Girls – Karen Lobodzic's)

(iii) Meet at the OLD ROCKFORD HOUSE at 8:30 p.m. Friday. (You can't miss it; there's a CRANE with a giant WRECKING BALL parked in front.)

(iv) Enter through missing planks in BOARDED-UP WINDOW, first floor, east side.

When a plan came from Griffin Bing, even the tiniest detail had to be perfect. He'd agonized over every fine point and possibility. All except one: What if nobody showed up?

"We probably shouldn't have put in the part about no TV," Griffin's friend Ben Slovak said glumly.

Griffin and Ben sat cross-legged on their sleeping bags in what had once been an elegant living room. They were surrounded by shredded drapery, remnants of ancient furnishings, and mounds of dust. All around them, the cavernous old house creaked and groaned with hollow, eerie noises. Outside, a thunderstorm raged.

Griffin trained the beam of his flashlight on his wristwatch: 10:34 p.m. "I can't believe it," he seethed. "How could we get *nobody*? Twenty-eight people said they were coming!"

"Maybe they're just late," Ben offered lamely.

"Nine o'clock is late. Ten-thirty is a no-show. Don't they have any self-respect? This is like saying it's totally fine for the adults in this town to walk all over us."

Ben would have dearly loved to be No-Show #29. Only loyalty to his best friend had brought him here tonight. "Come on, Griffin," he reasoned. "What difference does it make if two people or two *hundred* people spend the last night in a condemned building? How does that show the adults that we're standing up for our rights? They're never even going to know about it."

"*We'll* know," Griffin said stoutly, sticking out his jaw. "Sometimes you have to prove to yourself that you're more than just a slab of meat under the shrink-wrap in your grocer's freezer. Why do you think I came up with the fake sleepover idea? I wanted to make sure everybody had an excuse to be here. That was the whole point behind the plan."

The plan. Ben groaned inwardly. It was the best thing about Griffin, and also the worst. Griffin Bing was The Man With The Plan.

"Maybe the other kids wanted to come, but they were scared," Ben suggested.

"Of what?" Griffin challenged. "Dust? The rain? A whole night with no TV?"

"This house is supposed to be haunted," Ben insisted. "You know the rumors."

"What rumors?" Griffin scoffed.

"How do you think it got abandoned in the first place? Old Man Rockford was in jail for cutting up his wife with a chain saw — that's what Darren said."

"When's the last time Darren's said anything that's been worth the air it took to blow it out of his big fat head?" Griffin exploded. "He also says he's distantly related to the Rockfords — with no proof whatsoever.

Besides, they didn't even have chain saws back in Old Man Rockford's time."

"They had railroads, though," Ben noted. "According to Marcus, the real murder weapon was a railway spike pounded into her skull."

Griffin wasn't buying it. "He's just pulling your chain. You know how he loves messing with people."

"But Pitch doesn't, and you know what she heard? The house is haunted by the spirit of a dog that the old man brought home from Europe after World War One. Or maybe it wasn't a dog."

Griffin rolled his eyes. "Then what was it? A Komodo dragon?"

Ben shrugged. "Nobody knows. But just a few days after it got to town, pets started disappearing. At first it was just little kittens and puppies, but pretty soon full-grown Saint Bernards were vanishing into thin air. And there were bones buried all around the house — only Rockford wasn't feeding his dog any bones."

A flash of lightning cast strange angular shadows through the boarded-up windows. Ben paused to let his story sink in. "The towns-people took the law into their own hands. They put rat poison inside a big steak and left it on the doorstep. It never occurred to them that if an evil spirit could live inside a dog, it could live inside something else, too — like a house!" He peered around at the shadowed walls, as if expecting to see something supernatural and hideous coming through.

"Oh, come on!" Griffin refused to be shaken. "There's no such thing as a haunted house."

"Well, Marcus heard the same story," Ben said with a sniff.

"No, he didn't," Griffin reminded him. "He heard the one about the railway spike."

"He heard *both*. And so did Savannah. Only in her version, it wasn't a dog. It was a baby."

"Why would the townspeople poison a baby?"

"They didn't. It got carried off by a chicken

hawk. But the baby's ghost put a curse on the house to take back all the years it never got to live. There was this schoolteacher — the first non-Rockford ever to live here. No one saw her again after the day she moved in — or maybe they did. People talked about an old, old woman peering out an attic window. But here's the thing: That schoolteacher was only twenty-three."

A gust of wind blew through the eaves, and an unearthly moaning sound echoed around them. Ben's head retreated turtle-like into his collar, and even Griffin paled a little.

"No offense, Ben, but shut up. You're starting to creep me out." Griffin panned the crumbling walls with his flashlight. "It's almost eleven. Nobody's coming. Gutless wonders."

"It's the railway spike," said Ben nervously. "That's got to be a splitting headache. Literally."

Griffin spread out his bedroll and lay back, standing his flashlight on its base like a miniature floor lamp. "Let's try to get some sleep. The sooner the sun rises, the sooner we can get out of this rat trap."

"Maybe we can leave now," Ben suggested hopefully. "Since nobody else came, they'll never know that we weren't here all night."

Griffin was horrified. "You mean *back down*?" These two words were not in his vocabulary.

"I don't want my years sucked away by some baby's ghost!"

"There's no such thing!" Griffin exclaimed.

"Who says you have to believe in ghosts to be afraid of them?" Ben challenged. "All right, fine. I'll sleep." He rolled over onto his side, pulling his knees to his chest. "But if I wake up eighty-five years old, you owe me twenty bucks."

"Deal."

They lay there in silence for what seemed like a long time, listening to the machine-gun rhythm of rain on the ancient slate roof.

Griffin stared up at a gaping hole in the ceiling that had once held a chandelier. "I hope you know how much I appreciate this. You're the only kid who had the guts to see it through."

His friend said nothing, so Griffin went on. "I mean it, man. The others — they talk a good game, but where are they? Darren dared half the sixth grade to come. He even made fun of us, said we'd wimp out. But who's the real wimp, huh, Ben?"

Ben's reply was slow, steady breathing. Almost like . . . snoring?

"Ben?"

Griffin sat up and peered at his friend. Ben was curled into a ball on his bedroll, fast asleep.

Griffin let out a low whistle of admiration. Creepy house, creepy night, and Ben was relaxed enough to doze off. He came off as a big chicken sometimes, but when it really counted, he was too cool for school.

It was harder for Griffin to settle down. Not because he was scared. Not at all.

Griffin stayed up because he was mulling over the reason he and Ben were camping out with dust bunnies and a century of supernatural speculation.

He was thinking about the *last* plan.

2

As soon as the town had announced the meeting to decide what would be done with the Rockford land, Griffin had spoken those five fateful words: "Let's work out a plan."

PROPOSAL FOR DEVELOPMENT
OF ROCKFORD SITE
Griffin Bing—Head Designer

(i) This PLAN, approved by the KIDS of CEDARVILLE, shows how the land of the old ROCKFORD HOUSE can be turned into a SKATE and ROLLER PARK, laid out according to DIAGRAM "A" below (Scale: 1 inch = 12 feet) . . .

With the help of Ben, a few classmates, and Mr. Martinez, their teacher, Griffin put together a formal presentation to make to the town council. But on the big night, the committee had refused even to hear their proposal. They had already decided on their own project: a Cedarville museum.

It still rankled Griffin. Not losing. Sure, that had been disappointing. But to be ignored completely, brushed off like a mosquito, just because you were young, was unbearable. That was why he was here now, in this ancient dying house. That was why *everybody* should have been here — every kid who was sick of counting for nothing in this town. It wasn't going to get a skate park built, but at least it would win them some pride.

Anyway, spooky, uncomfortable, and boring as this was for Griffin, it had to be better than lying in bed at home listening to Mom and Dad arguing about money.

He regarded Ben's slumbering form with

envy. Try as he might, Griffin was too keyed up to fall asleep.

At last, he began to wander the empty husk of the Rockford house, his flashlight guiding him down hallways and through rooms. At least the thunder had passed, the storm settling into a steady rain. So much for a dark and stormy night.

And then the creature landed in Griffin's hair.

Full-on terror rocked him. The flashlight dropped from his hand, and the room was plunged into sudden darkness. He slapped desperately at his head as the attacker beat its scalloped wings, burrowing into Griffin's thick curls, squeaking and screeching. In his frenzy, Griffin tripped over his own flashlight and went down, wrapping himself in cobwebs as he rolled wildly around on the floor. He touched short fur, rubbery skin, and sharp clinging claws, but his slippery assailant resisted his grasping fingers.

It was over as unexpectedly as it had begun. The creature managed to disentangle itself and flew off, leaving Griffin writhing there. He retrieved his light just in time to see a large black bat fluttering up the open stairwell.

You're okay, he told himself, heart thumping. *Maximum gross, minimum danger.*

He frowned. There, illuminated in the cone-shaped beam, was a piece of furniture. Most of the house had been emptied prior to demolition day. Yet here was some kind of old-fashioned desk.

He scrambled to his feet and went over to investigate. It wasn't exactly *Antiques Roadshow* quality. It was beaten up and cracked, and the rolltop was stuck at an odd angle. By the glow of the flashlight, Griffin played with the many drawers and compartments. There was nothing of interest — just dust and the occasional dead spider.

One tiny drawer wouldn't budge. Griffin pulled and the knob came off in his hand. He tried to pry his fingers behind the face of the drawer, but there was zero movement.

He perched on the edge of the blotter to catch his breath. The seat of his jeans pressed against a small button.

Snap! The locked drawer popped open.

A release switch! This must be some kind of hiding place!

Eagerly, he shone the light inside the narrow compartment. Empty.

No, wait —

At the very back of the drawer, a flash of color caught his eye. He reached in and drew out an old faded card. There was a picture of a loaf of bread in the center, surrounded by the message: TOP DOG BAKERY PRODUCTS — FOR THE SANDWICH OF CHAMPIONS.

He turned it over and examined the other side.

There was a color drawing of a baseball player shouldering a bat. The image wasn't detailed, but the face seemed familiar. Griffin read the name at the bottom:

GEORGE HERMAN (BABE) RUTH

A baseball card! And it had to be old, too, since Babe Ruth had played a very long time ago. Griffin was no expert, but everyone knew that some old baseball cards were worth a lot of money.

Money — just the thought of it brought a dull ache to his stomach. The Bing family was really struggling to make ends meet these days. It had gotten so bad that Mom and Dad were even talking about selling the house and moving to a more affordable neighborhood.

"No way," Griffin said aloud, teeth clenched. It had taken him eleven years to break in this town and these friends. He wasn't about to give that up without a fight.

And if this card turned out to be valuable . . .

Get it out of your head, he admonished himself. What were the odds that someone would leave a priceless collectible to be destroyed inside a condemned building?

Still, it was possible. He could *hope* . . .

He made a face. Griffin was not a hoping kind of guy. His philosophy: If you want something, you *make* it happen. You don't sit around wishing for it to come true.

Yet the tantalizing image would not let go of him — his family's financial problems over, no more dark circles under his parents' eyes from staying up half the night, trying to squeeze money out of a bank account that had none to give. . . .

Even The Man With The Plan could be a dreamer when there was so much on the line.

3

The roar of a big motor jolted Ben out of a deep sleep. He sat bolt upright, rubbing eyes that seemed cemented shut. This wasn't his bed. Where was he?

The engine noise was so intense that he felt the churning in his stomach.

What makes a sound like that? A garbage truck? A semi? Or maybe . . .

He managed to focus enough to take in the sight of the dilapidated parlor around him.

. . . a crane carrying a giant wrecking ball!!

"Griffin!"

A shape stirred inside Griffin's sleeping bag.

Ben tore open the zipper to reveal his slumbering friend. "Griffin — wake up!"

"Wha —?"

"It's morning! *They're tearing down the building!*"

Griffin popped up like a champagne cork. "Let's get out of here!" he cried.

The two scrambled for the window. The entire house was vibrating with the clamorous thrum of the crane. Griffin got there first and stuffed the two sleeping bags and then Ben through the missing planks. He was halfway out himself, his stomach over the sill, when he realized he couldn't move forward or backward.

"I'm stuck!" he hissed.

Ben grabbed him by the wrists and hauled with all his might, but Griffin remained hung up in the opening.

A tremendous crash shook the structure and the very earth beneath Ben's feet. The impact pitched Griffin out the window, sending him sprawling on top of Ben. The two scrambled up, dazed. Griffin was white with plaster dust from the waist down.

"Run!" he bellowed.

They fled, the sleeping bags trailing behind them. As they rounded the corner, a chilling sight met their eyes: the titanic wrecking ball, buried deep in the shattered front of the old Rockford house.

If they needed any more reason to get away from there, it came from the horrified job foreman. "Hey, you! This is an active demolition zone!"

Coach Nimitz would have been amazed by the speed and stamina of their escape, which were much greater than they ever showed in gym class. The two kept up a lung-searing sprint for several minutes, spurred on by a series of loud booms behind them. They were halfway across town before Griffin pronounced the coast clear enough to slow to a walk.

"The next time you get a brilliant idea like spending the night in a death trap," Ben panted, "pretend my number is unlisted." In the distance, there was a long low rumble, followed by an earth-shaking thump. "That was almost us, you know. My mother didn't raise me to be rubble."

"No risk, no reward," said Griffin, catching his breath.

"Some reward. We got revenge on the town for our skate park — only nobody knows about it but us."

Griffin pulled the Babe Ruth card out of his pocket and waved it under his friend's nose. "Read it and weep." He gave Ben a quick recap of the discovery in the secret drawer.

"Babe Ruth — wow. Do you think it's real?"

Griffin shrugged. "It makes sense. Old house, old card. The question is, what's it worth?"

"But, Griffin — it's not yours," Ben whispered.

Griffin indicated the plume of dust that swirled in the air several blocks behind them. "When you knock down a house, you're really just throwing it in the garbage. It's not stealing to take something out of the garbage, is it? Besides —" He regarded the card ruefully. "*The Sandwich of Champions*? It's probably not valuable. I never get *that* lucky."

"How can you find out for sure?" asked Ben.

"There are experts in this kind of thing."

Ben's eyes widened. "Palomino's Emporium?"

Griffin smiled bravely. "We'll get an appraisal."

Palomino's Emporium of Collectibles and Memorabilia was a fortress unto itself. It was located just past the main strip of town in a low building surrounded by a high chain-link fence that always made Griffin think of a prisoner-of-war camp. It had once been a stone-cutter's workshop. As young children, he and Ben had always been fascinated by the display of grave markers in the small courtyard. Now the headstones had been replaced by sickly grass and a large dog, who was thankfully asleep.

Griffin indicated the front door.

VINTAGE ITEMS BOUGHT & SOLD
BEST PRICES GUARANTEED
S. WENDELL PALOMINO, OWNER AND
PROPRIETOR

Although they lived less than a mile away, this was their first time inside the store. Kids almost never came here. It was more like a museum than a comic shop — a museum where you could look but not touch, and everything was under surveillance by grim-faced guards. There were no rows of shelves cluttered with books, toys, knickknacks, cards, and souvenirs. In Palomino's Emporium, everything was frozen into its own glass case, with harsh lighting and security wiring. The whole place felt about as welcoming and warm as a bank vault.

Ben leaned into one of the displays to see an action figure and gaped at the sticker. "Six hundred and forty bucks? Are they crazy?"

A tall, cadaverous man with a ring of white hair around a bald crown walked over to him. "That's because it's a genuine 1966 Mr. Spock doll from the classic *Star Trek* TV series, still in its original packaging."

Ben frowned. "What kid has six hundred dollars to spend on a toy?"

"Exactly," the man agreed. "This isn't a toy store. Rare collectibles aren't for kids. They're a serious investment."

"Are you Mr. Palomino?" Griffin asked him.

"I'm Tom Dufferin, the assistant manager." He stretched out a bony arm and indicated another man, who was behind a long counter, inserting comic books into precisely sized protective sleeves. "That's the big boss over there."

S. Wendell Palomino was short, stocky, and surprisingly young — in his mid-thirties,

Griffin guessed, not nearly as ancient as Tom Dufferin. His curly hair almost (but not quite) fit underneath a New York Rangers cap. Thick glasses made his eyes appear twice their size, like two eggs, sunny-side up. He turned those eggs on his sixth-grade visitors. "What can I do for you, young gentlemen?"

Griffin pulled out his Babe Ruth card. "I'm thinking of selling this. I hear you guarantee the best prices."

The owner extended a pudgy hand and accepted the last surviving piece of the Rockford estate. His bushy eyebrows shot straight up to the Rangers logo on his hat.

Griffin was immediately alert. "It's valuable?" he asked.

Palomino laughed shortly. "Well, it would be — if it was real. You see, a lot of the old card series were reissued in the sixties and seventies. This one — the Top Dog Bakery line — was knocked off in 1967. I've seen a couple of these before, but not in a long time. Excellent quality reproduction." He held the card under a large magnifying glass attached to the counter. "You see this solid blue border? That was striped in the original. They weren't allowed to make an exact replica, because that would have violated counterfeiting laws. That's how we know it's a copy."

Ben took in the crestfallen look on Griffin's face. "Nineteen-sixty-seven was a long time ago," he said hopefully. "So it's still a little bit valuable, right?"

"Absolutely," the collectibles dealer confirmed. "Why, I saw a whole set of these once go for fifteen hundred dollars. But a single card like this — well, I'm a sucker for the Bambino. I'll give you a hundred bucks for it."

Griffin sighed, his visions of solving the family's money woes popping like soap bubbles. Still, he was a born negotiator. "A hundred and fifty," he said instantly.

Palomino chuckled. "You drive a hard bargain, sonny boy. Tell you what — one twenty."

"Sold."

The dealer counted out six crisp twenty-dollar bills from a thick roll and accepted the card in return. The boys peered over the counter as he stooped to turn the dial of a portable safe on the floor at his feet. He opened the door and locked his new acquisition inside.

Griffin frowned. "If the card isn't valuable, how come you need to keep it in a safe?"

"This isn't Toys 'R' Us, sonny boy," lectured Palomino, out of breath from the simple act of straightening up. "We take security seriously at Palomino's Emporium. A baseball card is the easiest thing in the world to swipe. Stick it in your pocket, and nobody even knows it's there. It stays in the lockbox until it's cataloged and ready for the display cases."

"Can't somebody just steal the whole safe?" Ben put in.

The dealer snorted. "You kids kill me. Steal the safe. That's funny."

Griffin spoke up for his friend. "He means it's not very big, and there's a handle on top. You could pick it up and walk out the door."

Palomino beckoned the two boys behind the counter. "All right, you guys. Give it a try."

Griffin and Ben took firm hold of the handle and pulled. The lockbox didn't budge.

"Come on." The dealer was grinning at them now. "Put some muscle into it!"

Grunting with effort, they pulled with all their might. Nothing.

Palomino burst out laughing in their faces. "It's bolted to the floor!"

Embarrassed, Griffin and Ben slunk out from behind the counter and headed for the door.

Tom Dufferin offered a sympathetic smile as they passed by. "You're not the first to try it. I doubt you'll be the last."

"Pleasure doing business with you, young gentlemen," Palomino called after them. "Come back any time."

As they passed the sleeping dog and

stepped outside the fence, both boys relaxed visibly. There was something unnerving about Palomino's Emporium — almost as if the store had its own energy field.

Ben took a breath of fresh air. "Sorry you're not rich."

In answer, Griffin took out his money, peeled off three of the twenties, and handed them to Ben. "Your cut," he said.

"I didn't do anything," Ben protested.

"Sure you did. You stuck with the plan when everybody else bailed."

That's how it was with Griffin. Always the plan — even when the plan had nearly gotten them buried under a building.

4

The light was on in the garage.

This was no big surprise — the light was *always* on in the garage. It was Mr. Bing's workshop. As long as Griffin could remember, his father had been tinkering with some invention in there. But never before had Dad become so obsessed with one of his creations that he'd quit his engineering job so he could develop it full-time.

The SmartPick™. Fruit picker of the future. When Griffin retreated to the garage later that afternoon to escape his parents' argument, the prototype lay on the workbench. Griffin pressed a button, and the telescoping aluminum shaft whirred outward. He worked the control in the opposite direction and the pole receded into itself.

There was nothing on the market like it. The FruitSafe™ picking mechanism used padded pincers and a twisting motion, rather than a cutting blade, for a zero-percent chance of damaged produce. It was a revolution in agriculture. Only . . .

Who needs a SmartPick when there are perfectly good human beings with real hands?

Griffin felt guilty for his disloyal thought, yet the common sense of it would not leave him alone. The Bings had bet their entire future on this so-called revolution. Otherwise, Dad would have kept his job, and nobody would be thinking about moving. It was thanks to the SmartPick that his parents were in the kitchen right now tearing their hair over some bill they didn't have enough money to pay. Their raised voices carried all through the house. Bickering, agonizing — sell A to pay for B, cut corners, spend less, economize, economize, economize.

And the worst part was that there was absolutely nothing Griffin could do about it. Here he was, The Man With The Plan, and he might as well have been a blob of Play-Doh for all he could help his family. He was too young to get a part-time job. He couldn't even hand over the sixty bucks from the Babe Ruth card without confessing the whole Rockford house escapade.

As he set down the SmartPick, the pole brushed against the antenna of his father's old black-and-white TV. For an instant, the ten-inch screen resolved itself into a very familiar face before returning to snow and interference.

Huh?

Griffin fiddled with the aerial until the picture returned. No, he wasn't seeing things. Grinning out at him were the unmistakable features of Babe Ruth. It was the baseball card from the old Rockford house!

He turned up the sound.

". . . when I bought the collection, I had no idea . . . but the instant I laid eyes on it . . . I mean, wow . . ."

Griffin recognized the breathlessness of the voice — like the speaker had just run a marathon.

The sunny-side-up eyes of S. Wendell Palomino appeared on the small screen.

What's a guy who sells overpriced Star Trek *dolls doing on TV?* Griffin wondered.

The dealer stood in the courtyard of Palomino's Emporium, holding up the Babe Ruth card for a group of reporters and cameramen.

"There are a lot of similar cards out there," one woman was saying. "What makes this one so special?"

"It was printed in 1920," Palomino explained, "Ruth's first season as a Yankee. But look at the picture —"

A cameraman zoomed in. "That's a Red Sox uniform," he observed.

Palomino nodded enthusiastically. "Right. The Top Dog Bakery people wanted to compete with the cigarette and chewing gum companies that dominated the baseball card market. The presses were already rolling before the trade went through. They were able to call back most of the run, but two hundred copies were released into circulation. Only a handful are known today. That's what makes this card especially valuable."

Griffin felt his blood boil. That liar, that *cheat*! He said it was a fake — a knockoff from the sixties! He invented a whole story about a solid border instead of a striped one!

"How much is it worth, Wendell?" another reporter piped up. "What are you selling it for?"

"Gentlemen, gentlemen." The dealer chuckled, obviously loving every minute. "This isn't the kind of item you slap a price tag on and stick in the window. The card will be sold to the highest bidder at Worthington's Annual

Sports Memorabilia Auction on October seventeenth. The opening bid will be" — he paused dramatically — "two hundred thousand dollars."

Griffin nearly choked.

The reporters were astonished.

"You think you can get that much?" asked a woman.

"I think I can get *more*," Palomino replied smugly. "Specimens from the famous T-206 set frequently sell for six-figure amounts. The legendary 1909 Honus Wagner card recently went for over two million. This misprint, showing the Bambino in a Red Sox uniform, is just as rare. The people at Worthington's think it could be the second card in history to break the million-dollar barrier."

A million dollars!

Griffin couldn't believe it.

It was right in the palm of my hands — enough to solve our money problems for life!

"I'm going over to Ben's!" Griffin hollered in the direction of the kitchen. He didn't wait for an answer from his parents, who were still wrangling over the checkbook.

An argument that wouldn't be happening if not for S. Wendell Palomino!

He jumped on his bike and pedaled down the driveway. He hoped Mom and Dad were too preoccupied to look out the window and notice that he was turning left, *away* from the Slovak house. He had another destination in mind.

He arrived at Palomino's Emporium just as the press conference was breaking up. The reporters and crew were filing out the opening in the fence, under the watchful eye of a Doberman pinscher.

"'Scuse me, kid." A soundman brushed past Griffin, bumping him with a microphone boom.

Suddenly, Griffin realized that he had no idea what he should do next. He may have been The Man With The Plan, but he had thought no further than getting himself to the store.

What could he say? *That's not his card, it's mine?* Technically, that wasn't true. Griffin had sold it and had been paid in full. Yes, Palomino had tricked him by implying that the card wasn't real. It was shady, underhanded, unethical, and even sleazy. But sleaze — by itself — wasn't against the law.

Besides, what if nobody believed him? He had no proof that he'd been the one to find the card, except for Ben's say-so. Adults didn't listen to eleven-year-olds. At the town meeting, they had refused to sit through a three-minute presentation about a skate park. Why would they accept the word of two kids when a million bucks hung in the balance?

When the media people had gone, Griffin ventured up to the store. The Doberman blocked the front door, its teeth bared. On top of everything else that was intimidating about this place, add one attack dog.

"That's okay, Luthor," came a voice from inside.

Reluctantly, the Doberman backed away, and Griffin entered. Palomino was in his usual spot behind the counter. With effort, he tore his attention from the baseball card in his hand. "What can I do for you, sonny boy?"

"You knew," Griffin accused him. "The minute I brought you that thing, you could tell it was no fake."

"Wait," the dealer said. "You're not saying that the piece of junk you sold me was *this* card? I found this in a collection I bought in an estate sale on the West Coast. Good luck — it happens. Somebody up there must like me."

"So where's *my* card?" Griffin demanded. "Show me my worthless piece of junk next to your Babe Ruth masterpiece."

"I already sold it. Took a bath on it, too. You were lucky I gave you as much as I did."

Griffin stared at him, blown away by the sheer dishonesty of the man. This wasn't some kid; it was an adult, the owner of a business. How could he act this way?

Palomino spoke once more. "A word to the wise: The world is a big fat scary place filled with people who'll chew you up and spit you out if you give them half a chance. Consider this your first life lesson."

"I came to you for a fair deal," Griffin sputtered.

"Oh, come down off your high horse." The dealer sneered. "You were after money, just like I was after money. Everybody's after money. Some of us are just a little better at it, that's all."

Griffin's eyes narrowed. "You won't get away with this."

Palomino laughed. "That's where you're wrong, sonny boy. You've heard that possession is nine-tenths of the law? In the collectibles game, it's *ten*-tenths of the law. If it isn't in your hand, you don't own it. Now get out of my store." He stuck a fat finger in his mouth and let out a sharp whistle.

With a growl that was more of a roar, Luthor burst into the shop. The Doberman sprang at Griffin, who backed away, colliding painfully with a display case of Yoda action figures. The big dog's snapping jaws were just inches from his trembling chin.

"Easy, Luthor," Palomino commanded with a chuckle. "Our friend was just leaving."

The dog withdrew a half step, but no more. Terrified, Griffin managed to sidestep the Yodas and retreat in the direction of the exit.

"We appreciate your business. Please do *not* come again," the dealer heckled gleefully as Griffin turned and ran out the door.

Back on his bike, Griffin struggled to wrestle his spinning thoughts into some kind of order.

(i) I've been CHEATED‼

Picturing the sentence as it might have appeared in one of his famous plans made him feel a little more in control. Cheated — that was exactly what had happened to him. And out of a lot more than a baseball card. A million dollars to develop the SmartPick. Even if the invention turned out to be a bust, that money would allow Dad to find a new job and start over. This was about the entire future of the Bing family!

It was time for The Man With The Plan to embark on the most important plan of his life.

But what could that possibly be? A lawsuit? The Bings could barely pay their mortgage. Where were they going to get money for lawyers?

No, there was only one way to get the card back.

Palomino had stolen it from him.

Griffin had to fight fire with fire.

B en's eyes very nearly popped out of their sockets. "You want to pull a *what*?"

"Shhh," whispered Griffin. It was lunch recess and the playground was crowded. "A heist."

"Like in the movies? A robbery? That's stealing!"

"Not stealing," Griffin amended. "Stealing *back*. There's a big difference."

"Are the police going to think so?"

"What would the police think about a store owner who rips kids off?" Griffin challenged.

"S. Wendell," Ben said with a sigh. "Never trust anybody whose name sounds like *swindle*."

"He's the *ultimate* Swindle," Griffin agreed. "He sure swindled me. And the only way to get that card back is to take it. What do you say?"

A hand came down on Ben's shoulder. "I say it's time for Mr. Slovak's allergy medication," announced Nurse Savage.

"Oh — right!" Ben exclaimed, startled. The last thing he wanted was for this robbery talk to be overheard by the school nurse. He began to follow her through a maze of whirling jump ropes.

Griffin grabbed his friend's wrist. "Hey, if your allergies are so bad," he asked in a low voice, "why weren't you sneezing from all the mold and dust in the old Rockford house?"

Ben shrugged. "Maybe the medicine really works."

Nurse Savage held open the door, and Ben disappeared inside the building.

"What the —?"

Something jagged scratched Griffin in the back of his neck. He wheeled around to find a sixth grader the size of an NFL linebacker stabbing at him with a long branch.

"Darren, what are you doing?" Griffin shouted.

"Can't you tell?" Darren Vader jeered, poking the stick at the bridge of Griffin's nose. "I'm field-testing my new invention, the DumbPick. Sorry, I thought your head was a coconut."

Angrily, Griffin slapped the branch away. "It's a SmartPick, you idiot, and it's a miracle of technology!" He would never have admitted his own doubts about his father's brainchild to Darren. "You wouldn't even know about it if you weren't such a snoop."

"I wasn't snooping," Darren defended himself. "My mom had the papers spread out on the kitchen table." Mrs. Vader was the lawyer who'd filed the SmartPick patent.

"Yeah, and way to blab it all over the school," Griffin accused.

"Excuse me for making sure a brilliant inventor gets some credit. You guys will be rich someday — you know, when millions of people decide to quit their jobs and start picking fruit."

"Shut up!" Griffin thundered. "You've always got so much to say, but when it comes to action, you're nothing! What about the old Rockford house, huh? Where were you on Friday night?"

"I had the flu," Darren mumbled.

"You don't look like you're at death's door."

"It was a twenty-four-hour bug!" Darren exclaimed.

"There was a lot of that going around." Griffin clucked disapprovingly, raising his voice to reach some of the other sixth graders nearby. "Nice show of solidarity, you guys — leaving Ben and me to stand up for the kids in this town."

"Sorry, Griffin," said Antonia Benson, who went by her climbing nickname, Pitch. "My family was at the indoor rock wall. I completely spaced."

"Me, too," admitted Marcus Oliver. "Totally blanked."

Griffin was unconvinced. "You guys didn't blank when it came to filling Ben full of stories about railway spikes and possessed pets."

"There's no such thing as a possessed pet," lectured Savannah Drysdale. "Animals are all innocent inside. And speaking of animals, that's why I couldn't be there on Friday. Madame Curie was about to litter. My hamster."

"And?" Pitch prompted.

"It was a boy," Savannah reported happily, "and another boy. And three girls."

"Well, I didn't miss it for any dumb reason like that," said Logan Kellerman haughtily.

"I have an audition for an acne cream commercial. I had to stay home and rehearse."

"Rehearse what?" Darren laughed. "Squeezing zits?"

"That shows what you know about acting. It's all emotion. The audience has to really believe my heartbreak over having a pimple."

"You *are* a pimple," Darren grunted.

"Whatever the reason, we're all sorry, Griffin," Pitch put in. "We shouldn't have flaked out on you that way. Maybe some of us *were* a little scared. Maybe we just didn't think it was worth it. Walking past that big pile of rubble this morning, I wished I had been there. Our loss."

"You bet it's your loss," Griffin said resentfully. But with the fruits of that adventure — the Babe Ruth card — in S. Wendell Palomino's chubby hands, he was in no mood to tell them why.

*   *   *

Mr. Martinez's students were working on their creative writing assignments when Ben got back to class. He deliberately avoided Griffin's searching eyes as he took the seat next to his friend.

"Let's get together after school to start work on the plan," Griffin whispered eagerly.

Every second he'd spent with the nurse, Ben had been dreading this conversation. Since the days when Griffin's plans had involved bicycles with training wheels, Ben had always been "in." It had become as constant as the sunrise. That was what made this so difficult.

"Griffin, I can't."

"Obviously we'll have to do some surveillance on the store," Griffin went on. "You know, pinpoint the weak spots —"

Ben wasn't even surprised that Griffin had missed his refusal. Once his friend was on a mission, nothing short of an earthquake would get his attention. "You're not listening, man. I can't do it. The answer is no."

That was earthquake enough. "What are you talking about?" Griffin asked. "Why not?"

Ben looked at him helplessly. "Where do I start? It's against the law, we'll never get away with it, and it's just plain wrong."

"It isn't wrong," Griffin said stoutly. "What Swindle did — *that's* wrong. We're just setting it right again."

"Okay, so it's not wrong. But it's wrong for *us*. We're not burglars. I know we talk about how kids can do anything adults can, but not this."

Griffin's voice rose in tone and volume. "Then Swindle *wins*!"

"Shhh," hissed Mr. Martinez from behind his desk.

"How can you let that jerk get away with taking advantage of us?" Griffin continued in a slightly lower voice. "How can you let him get *rich* doing it? That's *my* card, *my* money.

Our money, because I was going to give you half!"

"I don't want to be rich," Ben shot back. "Okay, maybe I do, but not this way."

"Boys — quiet," the teacher said warningly.

"I have to do this," Griffin pleaded. "I can't explain, but there's a good reason. Of all my plans, this one is the most important!"

"You always say that! Every plan is the most important — till the next one comes along!"

"This time it's true!" Griffin exclaimed. "The money —"

"Griffin and Ben," Mr. Martinez interrupted angrily. "Since you can't work quietly as neighbors, you're going to have to move. Ben, you go over and sit with Logan. Griffin — take the empty desk behind Melissa."

"But, Mr. Martinez —" Griffin began.

"*Now.*"

As he gathered up his papers, Griffin looked

beseechingly at his best friend. He mouthed the word, *"Please."*

Ben could barely muster the strength of will to shake his head no.

Griffin's despair was total. Year in and year out, there had always been one constant, one thing that could be relied on through floods and asteroid strikes: the unchanging fact that Ben was willing to follow him anywhere.

Yet today, with so much at stake, his loyal friend had let him down.

He had never felt so helpless.

*L*ogan Kellerman is an idiot.

That was the conclusion Ben had reached after three days of sitting next to the boy. The audition for the acne cream commercial had not gone well, and Logan could think of nothing else. He slumped at his desk, his already long face drawn out to banana-like proportions, blaming his failure on everybody except himself — the casting director, his parents, and Sanjay Jotwani.

"Who's Sanjay Jotwani?" asked Ben without interest.

"Only the greatest acting coach ever to come out of India," Logan told him. "He's giving private lessons in the city. Guess whose parents are too cheap to pay for it."

Ben cast a longing gaze across the classroom where Griffin sat behind Melissa Dukakis. That was what really bothered Ben, why he had so little patience for Logan's nonsense. The punishment was over. Mr. Martinez said the two were free to return to their old seats. But Griffin was so upset over Ben refusing to take part in the baseball card robbery that he wouldn't move.

"I don't sit with traitors" had been Griffin's declaration when Ben had made an attempt to come back.

Those were the only words Ben had heard from his best friend in the past three days. The icy silence between them had become so obvious that the other kids were starting to mention it. Pitch kept asking what was wrong, and even Darren commented, "Who broke up the Doofus Patrol?"

How could Ben ever explain it? The same dogged go-getter qualities that forged The Man

With The Plan made Griffin as stubborn as a mule when he was angry about something.

"Kate Mulholland has been working with Sanjay Jotwani for less than two months, and already she's landed a part in a heartburn commercial," Logan was lamenting. "I'm better than Kate Mulholland. I can do heartburn. I can do gastric distress. I can do constipation like nobody's business."

At least Griffin wasn't exactly having a picnic on the other side of the room with Melissa. She had a reputation as a computer genius, but it was impossible to be sure about that. She was the shyest kid in town, and spent most of her time hiding behind long stringy hair that completely covered her face.

As Ben watched, Melissa agitated her head until the curtain thinned to reveal pale skin and wide eyes. She mumbled a one-word answer to Griffin's question.

With a loud sigh, Logan put his books away and laid his head down on his desk. "What's the use? Who can think when my entire career is falling apart? My parents are way too East Coast to understand what it takes to make it in Hollywood."

Ben closed his eyes and pictured himself in a faraway place, where there was no such thing as a million-dollar baseball card, and heists only happened in action movies.

So this was what ex-friendship was like: Griffin was stuck with a kid who barely opened her mouth, and Ben was stuck with one who never shut up.

As miserable as sixth grade had become, the after-school hours were even worse. Ben was used to spending all his spare time with Griffin, so he wasn't just depressed; he was bored. A toxic combination.

He had been biking a lot, almost as if he believed he could outrun his loneliness if he pedaled hard enough. He must have passed the site of the former Rockford house a dozen times. The debris had been cleared away. All that remained was the stone foundation and the old-fashioned mailbox out front — a grave marker for the ghosts and murderers that had probably never lived there.

The place made him think of Griffin, just like every place made him think of Griffin. For Ben, very few landmarks in town didn't hold some special Griffin connection — the school, the town hall, Palomino's Emporium. It wasn't very long before he found himself on Griffin's street, almost as if his bike knew the way and had ridden there on its own. How often in the past had he wheeled up this block, turning onto the familiar driveway?

A woman he didn't recognize was on the front lawn, hammering in the stake of a cardboard sign. Ben squinted to read it:

FOR SALE

He was never sure exactly how he and the bike separated. The next thing he knew, he was flying through the air. He landed hard on the road, leaving much of the skin of his left elbow on the concrete curb.

The sign lady rushed over and helped him up. "Are you all right?"

Ben hardly noticed the pain or his bleeding arm. "This house isn't for sale!"

"It just listed this morning," she told him. "Do you need me to drive you somewhere? Is your mother home?"

Ben yanked himself away. "People live here!"

The door opened and Griffin peered outside. "Ben?"

Ben pointed to the woman. "She's trying to sell your house out from under you!"

"It's okay, Mrs. Brompton," Griffin told her. "He's my friend." He hustled Ben inside to the bathroom and held his injured arm under running water. "Calm down, man. She's our real estate agent."

"Real estate agent?" Ben pulled back from the sink, splattering the floor with pink-tinged water. "You mean your house really *is* for sale? You're moving?"

Griffin nodded.

"All because I wouldn't do the heist?"

"Of course not. Listen . . ." Griffin hadn't told a soul about the Bing family's financial problems. Now Ben listened with rapt attention.

"That's why I got so freaked out about the Babe Ruth card," Griffin concluded the whole sad story. "That money would save our house. It would let my dad develop his dream. It would change everything for my family. How can I let a sleazy two-bit con man take all that away?"

"I — I don't know what to say," Ben managed. As awful as these past few days had been, it was nothing compared to what Griffin must have been going through. No wonder he was so obsessed with the heist. He was fighting for his home and family.

Despite his horror at the thought of Griffin moving away, Ben was aware of an even stronger emotion. He'd always wondered what it would be like to be Griffin. To experience the pure, clear sense of purpose that was at the core of his friend's character. In that instant, all his doubts and misgivings about the robbery burned away. What was left was the searing certainty that this was not just the right course of action, but the *only* course of action.

"You really think we can pull off a heist?" Ben asked.

The Man With The Plan grinned.

THE GREAT BASEBALL CARD HEIST

Plan of Attack:

(i) Gain access to SWINDLE'S STORE

(ii) Locate SAFE behind SALES COUNTER

(iii) Burn HOLE in side of SAFE using Dad's BLOWTORCH

(iv) Return home RICH

Major Obstacles:

(i) Padlocked GATE

(ii) 7-foot-high FENCE

(iii) SECURITY GLASS on front DOOR

(iv) 3 DEADBOLTS

(v) Burglar ALARM – (How can we learn KEYPAD CODE?)

(vi) The X-factor – (Anybody who wires display cases and bolts a safe to the floor must have a few SURPRISES up his SLEEVE.)

Surveillance Report:

(i) Store hours: 10 a.m. to 6 p.m.

(ii) SWINDLE leaves 5:30 in black HONDA ELEMENT

(iii) Assistant Manager TOM DUFFERIN closes shop at . . .

7

"Six o'clock on the nose," Griffin hissed excitedly, making a note on his pad.

The two boys were hidden inside a large globe cedar directly across Ninth Street from Palomino's Emporium.

"Come on, Griffin. How about a little wiggle room?" Ben complained. "I've got a prickly branch up my armpit."

They watched as Dufferin got into a car parked at the curb. Griffin wrote down the make and model as the assistant manager drove away.

The two boys emerged from the bush, shaking and stretching cramped limbs.

"What do you think about the fence?" Griffin mused.

"I think it's a fence around a locked store with a burglar alarm," Ben confirmed. "Piece of cake — if you're made of ectoplasm and can walk through walls."

"Just because we haven't figured it out yet doesn't mean it can't be done," Griffin replied. "If you want it bad enough, it'll come to you."

They crossed the street and stood before the heavy chain that held the gate shut.

"Can we climb it?" Experimentally, Griffin jammed a toe in the mesh and hoisted himself up.

Luthor came out of nowhere. The big Doberman launched itself through the air and slammed into the fence opposite Griffin. The shocked boy lost his grip and tumbled into the arms of a terrified Ben. The two of them landed flat on their backs on the sidewalk. The monster clung to the mesh by its powerful teeth, snarling and growling.

Griffin hauled Ben upright, and they scrambled back across Ninth Street to the cover of their bush.

Griffin pulled out his notebook and wrote ANIMAL CONTROL?! in large letters across the page.

"Control *that* guy?" Ben squeaked. "I'd settle for not being his lunch."

Griffin looked thoughtful. "Who knows more about animals than anybody else in town?"

8

Savannah Drysdale was talking to a rabbit.

She whispered softly into a floppy ear as she held the animal on her lap, rocking slowly on her frilly purple quilt. Griffin and Ben could not make out what she was saying, but it was obvious that the creature was totally calm in her arms.

Mrs. Drysdale cleared her throat. "Savannah." Louder: "Savannah, your friends are here." She disappeared into the hall.

Savannah regarded them dubiously, but she set the rabbit down. It hopped over to an elaborate cage in the corner, where it shared a water-feeding tube with a pair of hamsters.

"I guess you have a lot of pets," Griffin observed.

"Not 'pets,'" Savannah replied pointedly. "In this house, we're all equal partners — my mom and dad, me, my brother, our dog, two cats, four rabbits, seven hamsters, three turtles, parakeet, and albino chameleon."

"If it's albino, how does it change color?" asked Ben.

"He has to stay white. It's a disability. And his name is Lorenzo, not 'it.'"

Griffin cleared his throat carefully. "That's really cool that you can talk to rabbits. Does it work with other animals that way?"

"We don't talk about the weather, if that's what you mean. Animals are sensitive to the tone of your voice, the vibe you put out. They know who to trust and who not to trust. They may not be able to understand your words, but they know they're safe with

you. It's not a conversation, but you're definitely communicating. Why?"

"We need you to talk to a dog," Ben
blurted.

Savannah's eyes narrowed. "What dog?"

"Remember what you said about how all
animals are innocent inside?" Griffin reminded
her. "Well, there's this guard dog on Ninth
Street, a Doberman — he's pretty much pure
T. rex. We're talking vicious, nasty, mean —"

"Stop right there," Savannah interrupted. "A
guard dog is only mean because that's how he
was trained. If you take a newborn puppy and
raise it so that the one behavior that ever gets
rewarded is aggressive, you're going to wind
up with a pretty rough adult dog."

"That's Luthor, all right," put in Ben.

"But that doesn't make it the dog's fault,"
Savannah continued sharply. "And it doesn't
mean that a little puppy isn't trapped in
there somewhere, waiting for a chance to
come out."

"What if the good dog's been trapped so long that it's gone forever?" Griffin wondered, laying it on thick to get to Savannah. "Then you're just left with one-hundred-percent bad dog. That's so *sad*."

"There's no such thing as one-hundred-percent bad dog," said Savannah with certainty. "You take me to this Doberman."

6:10 p.m. As Tom Dufferin drove away from Palomino's Emporium, Griffin and Ben emerged from an alley, escorting Savannah to her meeting with Luthor.

"He's spectacular," she whispered at her first sight of the Doberman, and then choked back a sniffle of emotion. "Sorry," she said, catching herself. "But what kind of a heartless person imprisons an elegant and noble animal behind a fence?"

"The kind who doesn't want his elegant and noble animal eating any pedestrians?" Ben suggested drily.

"He's kidding," Griffin put in quickly. "The guy whose store this is — he runs a simple comic shop like a military base. You should see the inside. Everything's locked away and alarm-wired." Griffin's outrage was genuine. Of all the places in town to break into, Palomino's Emporium had to be the most treacherous.

Savannah nodded grimly. "To him, this beautiful dog is just another *Keep Out* sign. We'll see about that. Luthor, sweetie," she called in a loving tone, "come and say hello. I'm a friend."

The Doberman stopped dead in its yard patrol and regarded her, its gaze oozing anything but friendship. A low rumble seemed to rise from its belly.

"You're right," she intoned to Griffin. "I can feel the resistance. The poor thing has been taught to be hostile and angry."

"No, you're doing great!" Griffin hissed. "When it was me, he tried to chew through the gate."

She took another step forward. The boys

did not accompany her. Luthor's ears went up. The growl got louder.

"I can't look," moaned Ben.

Savannah glared at him. "You're ruining everything. A living creature has a sophisticated radar that can sense the emotions around him. Your negativity is spooking him."

"Godzilla couldn't spook that dog," Ben mumbled, backing away.

Savannah unzipped a small duffel bag and produced a hard rubber toy in the form of a pink poodle with voluminous fur and a pom-pom tail.

Griffin frowned at it. "What's that supposed to be? His long-lost brother?"

"Part of the cruelty of a guard dog's training is the way his world becomes all confrontation and conflict," Savannah explained. "We have to bring out the playful side of his personality, which has been suppressed for so long. The imagination, the whimsy, the fun." She turned to the Doberman, smiling encouragingly. "Here,

Luthor. I've brought something for you." She gently lobbed the poodle over the fence.

It never reached the ground. With a blood-curdling roar, Luthor leaped into the air and intercepted the gift with snapping, tearing jaws.

The poodle was dismantled in a matter of seconds. And there stood the Doberman at the center of a scattering of pink rubber shreds. The scene looked like someone had fed a box of erasers through a jet engine.

"Wow," Griffin managed in awe.

Savannah nodded her agreement. "What a magnificent animal!"

Magnificent was not the word Griffin and Ben would have chosen.

While Savannah made nightly visits to the store in an attempt to reach Luthor's inner puppy, Griffin and Ben turned their attention to Swindle's burglar alarm.

For three straight days they spent the after-school hours in the Slovaks' den, squinting at the plasma TV. Their noses were pressed to the screen as they painstakingly followed the path of a huge finger.

"I see blue spots in front of my eyes," Ben complained.

"You're lucky," Griffin told him. "I can barely see at all. Come on, we've almost got it."

It had been Griffin's idea to secretly video-tape Tom Dufferin punching in the alarm code. Then they could work out the numbers from the movement of the assistant manager's hand. Over the past seventy-two hours, the boys had memorized his every hangnail and skin wrinkle. But the four-digit sequence continued to elude them.

Griffin backed up the tape and ran it again. "I think the first and last numbers might be one. See? The finger's at the top left. And the third is probably zero — it's at the very bottom of the pad. That leaves just the second number."

"It's in line with the one, only lower down," Ben observed. "What's under one on a keypad?"

"Four or seven. So it's either *one-four-zero-one* or *one-seven-zero-one*."

"If we guess wrong, the alarm will bring every cop in town down on our heads," Ben said nervously.

With a sigh, Griffin paused the tape. "So how's Savannah coming along with Luthor?" Supervising the evening sessions at the fence had become Ben's job while Griffin crafted the rest of the plan.

"Terrible," Ben reported. "At this rate, we won't have to worry about the alarm. We're both going to be torn to pieces before we get to the door."

"No better than last time?"

"The barking isn't quite as loud," Ben offered. "But that's only because she's feeding it peanut butter treats, and I think its mouth is glued shut. If the gate wasn't there, it would spit out the treats and eat Savannah."

"She says she can do it," Griffin insisted.

"The dog just has to let down its guard and trust her."

"I feel kind of lousy tricking her into this," Ben admitted. "She probably has better ways to spend her nights than kneeling at a fence trying to sweet-talk a ferocious beast."

"We'll give her a share of the money from the Babe Ruth card when we get it," Griffin promised.

"You sure you boys can see from there?" came a voice.

Startled, Ben reached for the remote, but it was too late. His father was already in the living room.

Mr. Slovak frowned. "What's this, some kind of homemade reality TV?"

Griffin spoke up. "It's a project for school. You have to guess the code." He hit the PLAY button on the VCR. "We've got it narrowed down to *one-four-zero-one* or *one-seven-zero-one*."

"School sure has changed since the days of the three R's," commented Ben's father. "I don't have a clue. Unless —" An odd expression appeared on his face. "Is there a chance your teacher might be a *Star Trek* fan?"

Griffin perked up. "Why?"

"People choose combinations that will be easy for them to remember. On classic *Trek* from the 1960s, the serial number of the USS *Enterprise* was NCC 1701." He looked embarrassed. "I know — I'm an old nerd."

Griffin thought back to the security cases of figurines, models, and toys at Palomino's Emporium. There had been merchandise from dozens of TV shows, movies, and fads of every variety. But sixties *Star Trek* seemed to be a favorite.

"Don't worry, Mr. Slovak," Griffin said, unable to keep the triumph out of his voice. "I think the guy we're dealing with might be an old nerd, too."

9

For Griffin, watching a plan coming together was like completing a jigsaw puzzle. It started as a flimsy frame on the outer edges, then slowly the pieces filled in until the final image began to appear. With the baseball card heist, however, the finished picture was marred by a gaping black hole named Luthor.

It was Savannah's fourth meeting with the Doberman, and the girl was still baffled. "I don't understand it," she confessed, leaning against the fence outside Palomino's Emporium. "I've fed him, soothed him, talked to him, reasoned with him. I watched *The Horse Whisperer* twice last night, hoping for inspiration."

"Maybe you should watch *Dog Whisperer*," Ben suggested glumly.

"I've already TiVo-ed the entire season," she replied earnestly. "Nothing helps. I never thought I could write off an innocent animal. But I have to admit it — this dog is beyond my reach."

Griffin was stricken. "You're giving up? No! You can't!"

She shrugged helplessly. "Believe me, it doesn't make me happy. But what choice do I have?" She indicated Luthor on the other side of the fence. "Look at his eyes. There's no letup in the anger. Not even any curiosity about me. This is my fourth night here, but to him I'm just an intruder."

Griffin was devastated. "You can't quit now!" he moaned. "Please, *please* give it one more shot!"

Savannah's look of disappointment morphed into deep suspicion. "Wait a minute. I know you guys. You're not getting this worked up over a dog. What's this really about?"

Griffin hesitated. The more people who were in on a conspiracy, the greater the chance that one of them would let something slip. But he had no choice. Without a dog whisperer to neutralize Luthor, any plan would be doomed.

There was no way to sugarcoat it, so he told her straight out, "We need you to calm down the dog so we can break into the store and steal a baseball card." Savannah's jaw dropped open in shock, so Griffin quickly stammered, "It's not as bad as it sounds! We'll give you a cut of the money!"

Her face burned bright red with fury. "I can't believe you just said that! You want me to help you pull off a robbery! You're either crazy or you think *I'm* crazy! I'm telling my mother! I'm telling Mr. Palomino! I'm telling the police!" As her voice rose, she gestured wildly, and a couple of fingers penetrated the chain-link fence.

Like a shark smelling blood in the water, Luthor snapped at her hand and would have taken off both digits if Ben hadn't pulled her back from the gate.

Her rage doubled, Savannah wheeled on the Doberman. *"You miserable mangy waste of dog food, how dare you do that to me? I've shown you nothing but kindness — and this is how you behave? You don't deserve to be an animal! Rabies would be too good for you! You should be put on a rocket ship and blasted to Alpha Centauri, you evil soulless ill-tempered psychopathic canine!!"*

Griffin and Ben were frozen in shock at the sudden change in their classmate. Never had they heard such a tirade — and certainly not from soft-spoken, levelheaded Savannah Drysdale.

But the boys' reaction was mild compared to the effect of the outburst on Luthor. The lunging beast tumbled off the fence as if it had suddenly become boneless. It dropped to its belly and began groveling toward Savannah, wagging its tail and whimpering, gazing up at her with soulful, pleading eyes.

"Savannah —" breathed Ben. "Look!"

"I'm never going to forgive you guys for this!" she hissed. "Do you think I wanted to take a proud, glorious animal and break his spirit?"

"It's okay!" Griffin insisted. "This is *exactly* what we were hoping for!"

"Now you see where crime gets you," she seethed. "Not only are both of you going to jail, but you've forced me to go against everything I've ever believed in! I've destroyed this beautiful dog!"

"This beautiful dog almost ate two of your fingers," Ben reminded her.

"Savannah — listen," Griffin said, "we're not criminals. That card is rightly ours —"

"I don't care!" Savannah interrupted hotly. "I'm leaving!" She reached through the fence and stroked the dark fur behind Luthor's neck. "I'm sorry, boy. I didn't mean to do it."

The Doberman rolled over, presenting its belly to be tickled.

Griffin was desperate. "Fine — you can leave. You can even hate our guts. But *please* don't tell anybody what we're planning!"

"No fear of that." Savannah was clearly both angry and hurt. "As far as I'm concerned, you two nut jobs don't even exist anymore! If you want my opinion, you should both seek mental help!" She kissed Luthor through the fence, promised "I'll come visit you, sweetie," and stormed off into the night.

Griffin watched her walk away. "Well," he said, "that could have been a lot worse."

Ben gawked at him. "I hope you're kidding."

"Think about it. She took care of the dog and promised not to rat us out. What more could we ask for?"

Luthor tossed them a baleful look and trotted off into the shadows near the store.

Ben was unconvinced. "I don't know, Griffin. He doesn't look so taken care of to me. What if the dog whispering only works for Savannah?"

Griffin shrugged. "You saw how to handle him. If he gets uppity, you just have to yell and scream and threaten to send him to Alpha Centauri. I've got that special feeling in my gut — and it says the time to act is now."

Ben frowned. Griffin's gut was as reliable as Old Faithful when it came to choosing the right time to put a plan into action. Only —

"We're not ready yet," he protested. "The plan isn't even finished. We still don't have a way to get past the dead bolts and into the store."

"Oh, yes we do." The Man With The Plan could not suppress a smile. "Remember that fifth-grade project on the Trojan War . . . ?"

10

On October tenth at exactly 5:30 p.m., S. Wendell Palomino left his store and drove off in his Honda Element. He never noticed two furtive eyes peering out of a narrow alleyway at the end of the block.

A moment later, Griffin teetered onto the sidewalk, struggling with a heavily laden hand truck. Balanced on the cargo ledge was a large crate that might have held a thirty-three-inch TV.

It did not hold a thirty-three-inch TV.

There was a grunt of pain as the hand truck bounced over a spot of broken pavement, and a voice from inside the box hissed, "Watch it!"

Griffin said nothing. In the Trojan War, talking to the warriors hidden inside the wooden horse was a definite no-no.

Twisting his neck to see over his shoulder, he backed down the street and peeked in the open gate in front of Palomino's Emporium. Perfect. No customers. Tom Dufferin was alone, tidying up the sales counter.

Griffin frowned. The assistant manager had a clear view of the door.

Come on, he thought. *Move.*

A minute passed. Then two. Sweat formed on Griffin's brow. How long could he stand here before someone noticed a thousand-pound crate in the care of an eleven-year-old deliveryman?

At last, Dufferin picked up an armload of comics and headed to a display case at the back of the shop.

Now!

Griffin nearly dislocated both shoulders tipping the load so he could roll it again. Ears roaring, he hauled the shipment in through the gate and set it down at the entrance.

Uh-oh. The hand truck was stuck under the weight of the container. He couldn't budge it.

"What's going on?" came an urgent whisper from the box. "What's all that shaking?"

"Shhh!" Griffin hissed.

Inside the store, Dufferin had finished shelving the comics. In another few seconds, he'd be back at the front.

Griffin marshaled his strength and gave a mammoth yank. With a screech, the cargo ledge pulled free. One of the metal handles whacked him in the mouth, and he staggered backward, tasting blood. Reeling, he scampered out through the gate.

It had been close, but he'd made the drop-off.

The operation had begun.

Tom Dufferin frowned at the bulky crate that had suddenly appeared at the door. He hadn't

83

heard the delivery truck. It must have come in the last few minutes, when he'd been in the back.

He examined the brown paper that covered the wooden frame. It bore the address of the shop and the message:

Attn: S. Wendell Palomino — Personal and Confidential
To Be Opened by Addressee *Only*

With a shrug, Tom dragged the heavy container inside. Idly, he wondered what was so special that Palomino himself had to open it. Printed matter, probably, judging by the weight — somebody's lifelong collection of comic books or magazines.

He set the store's alarm, stepped out, and locked the door behind him. Whatever it was, the boss would deal with it when he arrived the next morning.

On the other side of the glass, the paper moved ever so slightly — the rustle of nervous breath through air holes.

There were times that Ben Slovak wished he had an ordinary best friend instead of The Man With The Plan. An ordinary best friend never would have convinced him to shut himself in a TV crate to get inside Palomino's Emporium. That was definite.

As Trojan horses went, the crate was a cramped affair. Ben was the smallest kid in sixth grade. Still, he had to lie on his side, with his knees pulled into his chest, to fit into the small space.

No pain, no gain, he reminded himself. *This is for a million bucks.*

For some reason, the money didn't seem quite real to him. Helping the Bings, saving them from having to sell their house — *that* was real. He'd do anything not to lose Griffin. But a million dollars for a baseball card? Science fiction.

Yet the weight of all that cash closed in on him as relentlessly as the frame of the crate.

Stealing something worth a million was the same as stealing the million itself, wasn't it? On top of everything else that made him uneasy about this caper, he couldn't escape the feeling that they might be committing a very serious crime.

He peered through the gloom at his watch — 6:03. Sundown was supposed to come at 6:57. After that, the plan added thirty minutes more to let it get dark. By that time, it would be impossible to read the dial.

"Count," Griffin had instructed.

Easy for him to say —

Eighty-seven minutes equaled 5,220 seconds. And . . . hey! Now it was 6:05. The first hundred and twenty seconds were already over. He could start at 121 . . . 122 . . . 123 . . .

Just before two hundred, he was aware of the first yawn. *Stop it*, he commanded himself. *Nobody falls asleep in the middle of a heist . . .*

Yet as he counted doggedly on, he could

feel his eyelids getting heavier, the way they always did.

No! Not here! Not now! He had barely reached five hundred.

"Five twenty-nine! . . ." His voice filled the empty store. "Five thirty! . . ."

This was crazy! Fear alone should be keeping him awake! Did Achilles get caught napping inside the Trojan horse?

"Eight hundred and one! . . . eight hundred and two! . . ."

He actually counted 803. But he was no longer awake to hear it.

11

"Here, Luthor. Where are you, boy?"

Griffin squinted through the gate into the darkness of the yard. The Doberman was nowhere to be seen.

Griffin frowned. Not that he had any great love for the dog. But it was always unnerving when real life didn't match what you'd planned for. What if Luthor had been left overnight in the store? If Ben opened the crate to find that ravening beast staring at him, he'd have a heart attack.

Anxiously, Griffin began to climb the fence. It was tougher than he expected because of the acetylene tank of his father's blowtorch, which was strapped to his back. He clambered down the opposite side and shined a flashlight through the display window. No sign of Ben *or* the dog. Griffin's eyes fell on the crate, which sat just inside the door. The wrapping paper was undisturbed.

He checked his watch. It was 7:45. Why was Ben still in the box? He rapped on the glass. "Ben!" he stage-whispered into the crack of the door. He knocked harder. "What are you doing, man? It's time!"

He experienced a moment of irrational terror. Had they forgotten the air holes?

And then the scissors broke through the brown paper. Griffin watched breathlessly as the blade sawed laboriously around the square frame and disappeared again. A moment later, the lid was pushed open, and Ben's head popped into view.

Griffin took in the bleary, blinking eyes. *He fell asleep?* Through his disbelief, Griffin couldn't suppress a hint of admiration. It was hard to imagine anyone being able to relax at a time like this. Ben was one in a million.

A beeping sound brought Griffin back to urgent focus. *The alarm!* The intruder had triggered the motion sensor.

Ben scrambled to the keypad. He had thirty seconds, no more. Griffin tried to fight off his uncertainty as his friend punched in 1-7-0-1. If they were wrong about the code, the siren was going to bust every eardrum between here and New York City.

There was a triple chime, and the beeping stopped. The alarm was off.

Ben unlocked the door and let Griffin inside. "Sorry I'm late," he said sheepishly. "Any problems with the dog?"

Griffin shone his flashlight up and down the aisles. "The dog's a no-show. Must be flea-bath night."

Ben looked around restively. "I hate this place. It's like the wiring of those cases is going to come alive and strangle us."

Griffin patted the blowtorch. "Forget the cases. All we want is the safe."

They followed the beam to the original scene of the crime — Swindle's sales desk. Griffin felt no guilt, only the exhilaration of a perfectly executed plan. They had done it. They were inside. No dog, fence, dead bolt, or burglar alarm could stop them now.

He moved behind the counter. And froze.

The lockbox was not there.

"Where's the safe?" he blurted.

Ben appeared at his side. "Behind the cash regis —" His mouth fell open.

"It was right here — attached to the floor!" Griffin got down on his knees and focused the flashlight on the weathered hardwood. Four bolt-holes marked the spot where the lockbox had once been.

"Search the store!" Griffin rasped.

They combed the aisles, the stock area, even the bathroom. The safe was nowhere to be found.

Griffin looked stunned. "I considered every possible move and countermove. Except one."

Ben nodded miserably. "A safe that can be bolted can also be unbolted. And taken someplace else."

Swindle had turned out to be a step ahead of them.

"A perfect plan, executed perfectly. And it's all for nothing."

"Maybe not," Ben said hopefully. "I mean, the card's not here. But we're standing in the middle of Swindle's store. So instead, why don't we just take a bunch of other stuff that adds up to the same money?"

Griffin swelled like a blowfish. "I am not a thief! I came here to find what's rightfully mine and take it back. I don't want anything that doesn't belong to me."

"But you'll never track down that card now," Ben reasoned. "Who knows where Swindle could have hidden it? It could be in a safe-deposit box in a bank vault."

Griffin could offer only a helpless shrug. There was no quit in him, no surrender. But without the slightest clue where the Bambino might now be, no amount of planning, or creative thinking, or even genius was going to make a particle of difference.

The Man With The Plan had run out of ideas.

12

Misery.

There was no other word for it. Watching Mrs. Brompton march an endless parade of house hunters through the Bing home was more than Ben could bear. He regarded each potential buyer with suspicion and outright hostility. Could these nice people be The Enemy? The ones who would force Griffin's family to move — who would split up the greatest pair of friends Cedarville had ever seen?

As awful as it was for Ben, it had to be even worse for Griffin. It was *his* life that was being turned upside down. And not just by real estate agents. His entire personality had changed. The fire was gone, along with the razor-sharp sense of purpose that had always guided him.

How many times had Ben prayed for a break from Griffin's never-ending schemes? Now he would have given his right arm to hear his friend burst out with "All right, here's the plan. . . ." To do something, *anything*! Whatever it was, it had to be better than treading water, waiting for the inevitable — an offer on the house, a deal, packing, moving. The end of Griffin and Ben.

At least it wasn't boring. The Bings were looking for reasons to be out of their home while it was being shown, so they were dragging Griffin — and Ben with him — to every mall, park, carnival, street fair, and free concert. On the surface he was having fun. Yet deep down, it was like trying to enjoy great food while suffering from a gut-blaster stomachache. It was hard to be entertained today when tomorrow seemed very little like entertainment. And anyway, all he could think about was yesterday.

The unsuccessful heist haunted the boys. The cleanup operation replayed itself in an endless loop in Ben's head. Ditching the empty TV crate, locking and re-alarming the store. Even wiping the fingerprints from the keypad and doorknobs had been a halfhearted effort. Who would call the police to investigate the disappearance of absolutely nothing? At the most, Tom Dufferin might wonder about the delivery that had mysteriously disappeared. More likely, he would assume that his boss had dealt with it. In a way, the operation had been the perfect crime — in and out without a trace. How could such a glorious success have been such a dismal failure?

They hashed and rehashed the details until their throats went dry. Only the roles were reversed. Ben was the one prodding *what now, what next?*

"You can't heist something if you don't know where it is," Griffin said sadly.

And it made total sense — in every way but one. Griffin Bing did not admit defeat. It was simply not in his DNA. How had he suddenly become The Man *Without* The Plan?

They were riding home from yet another concert in the Bings' van when the barking sounded — not the playful yelp of a house pet, but a full-throated braying.

"Goes to show how I've got Swindle on the brain," Griffin mumbled unhappily. "For a minute there, I could have sworn I heard Luthor."

Ben peered out the rear window. A large black dog was chasing them. "I don't think that's even a Doberman. . . ." As they left their pursuer yowling stubbornly in the road, a thoughtful expression appeared on Ben's face. "Wait a minute! It wasn't Luthor — but it *could have been*!"

Griffin regarded him oddly. "It could have been my grandmother, too. It wasn't. What are you talking about?"

"Don't you get it? The real Luthor has to be *somewhere*! He wasn't at the store on heist night. Where was he?"

Griffin gave a listless shrug. "At home, I guess. Swindle probably gave him a few days off threatening people at Palomino's Emporium. It's no big deal. The card isn't even there anymore."

"Think," Ben ordered. "What if Luthor's absence and the card's absence are connected?"

"Don't talk in riddles, man!"

"Luthor's a *guard* dog," Ben reasoned. "When the Bambino was at the store, so was Luthor. But if Swindle brought Luthor home —"

Light dawned on Griffin. "The card is at Swindle's house!"

When they reached the Bings', Griffin and Ben made a beeline for the phone book.

"Please let the guy live in town!" Griffin threw the directory open to the Ps — more specifically, *Palomino, S. W.*

There was the address: *531 Park Avenue Extension.*

"That's not too far from the store!" Ben exclaimed breathlessly. "We did it, Griffin! We figured out where the card is!"

Griffin nodded, his cheeks flushed with purpose. "Now all we need —"

Ben finished his sentence. "Is a plan."

"Not just any plan. This time we need the *ultimate* plan."

13

SWINDLE'S HOUSE – 531 PARK AVENUE
EXTENSION

(i) Two-story HOME, steep-pitched ROOF

(ii) Chain-link fence – even higher than at store

(why me?)

(iii) No neighbor in BACK, town WATER TOWER

(iv) PRIVATE PROPERTY signs (2)

(v) NO TRESPASSING signs (3)

(vi) KEEP OUT signs (4)

(vii) BEWARE OF DOG signs (6)

"**S**windle sure loves signs," Ben observed nervously.

"He loves chasing people away," Griffin amended. He frowned at a sticker on one of the door sidelights:

THESE PREMISES PROTECTED BY AN ULTRATECH SENTRY-MAX™ SECURITY SYSTEM WITH WIRELESS RADIO TRANSMITTER FOR INSTANT POLICE ALERTS

"Great," he muttered. "Another alarm."

"And this one looks like something out of a James Bond movie," Ben added. His eyes fell on a dog dish on the stoop and a leash handle wrapped around the wrought-iron railing. Heart sinking, he tracked the leather leash through the bushes and around the side of the house. The taut line went suddenly slack. "Uh-oh."

Ben was already in motion before they heard the first bark. He grabbed a bewildered

Griffin and began dragging him across the lawn.

Luthor exploded from behind the house in a pose that had become all too familiar — a ravenous predator in pursuit of prey.

"The road!" Griffin rasped.

The two flung themselves over the curb a split second before Luthor ran out of leash and was yanked back by his collar. A motorcycle swerved to avoid the boys as they pounded across the street. The Doberman twisted and writhed, howling its outrage.

"I guess we'd better tell Savannah that her dog whispering is only temporary," Ben panted.

A slow chuckle mingled with Luthor's angry braying. Griffin turned to notice an elderly neighbor in a rocking chair on the porch of number 530. The man was peering at them over his reading glasses with great interest.

"Haven't seen you two around before. New in town?"

Griffin hesitated. It would be risky to say yes. Just because he didn't recognize the old guy didn't mean he might not be a friend of a friend of Griffin's family. Cedarville was, after all, a fairly small community.

"We're experimenting with some new ways home from school," he replied. "Bully problems."

The man's face darkened. "Kids today. You wouldn't believe the things I see just sitting in this very chair!"

Griffin swallowed hard. The chair was perfectly positioned to watch the neighborhood in both directions. The Palomino front door was dead ahead, across the street.

"Spend a lot of time out here?" he asked faintly.

"Every waking minute," the man said cheerfully. "I worked forty-three years down in the coal mines. In my book, a second out of the fresh air is a second wasted."

"Even in bad weather?" Ben ventured.

"I dress for it. Rain or shine, hot or cold, Eli Mulroney is right here."

"Except at mealtimes," Griffin prompted.

"That's what a microwave is for," Mr. Mulroney said agreeably. "So I don't have to waste time cooking. Got no TV and no computer. Plenty of top-notch entertainment right out here. Like watching you two hotfooting it across the road with Luthor on your tail." He treated himself to a good laugh. "Think you were better off with the bullies. At least they don't bite."

Griffin and Ben tried to laugh with him.

"What kind of people have a dog like that?" Griffin complained. "Doesn't it, you know, attack the mailman, or bite their kids?"

"Hah! If there's anyone nastier than that dog, it's the fine fellow who owns it. He lives solo — who'd bunk with a creep like that? But Luthor's not around much. 'Pal-o-mine' usually has the critter on guard duty at his store. Wonder why the monster's here all of a sudden. Probably ate a few customers in the shop."

Griffin felt some small measure of satisfaction. Eli Mulroney may have been the unofficial CIA of Park Avenue Extension, but the old man still didn't know the real reason Swindle had moved Luthor from store to home. Griffin was sure of it: The safe was there, with the card inside it.

He grimaced. Bad enough Swindle was a security freak with an attack dog and an alarm system that had everything short of laser cannons. How were they supposed to pull off a heist under the nose of a full-time neighborhood spy?

*   *   *

**WWW.ULTRATECH.USA
MILITARY-CALIBER SECURITY
FOR YOUR HOME**

Griffin leaned back from the computer screen, whistling nervously through his teeth.

"How bad?" asked Ben.

They were in the school library, researching S. Wendell Palomino's security system, hoping to find a way to beat it.

"You know what the UltraTech company is?" Griffin groaned. "They take the alarms the navy used to put in dry-docked submarines and install them in people's houses. Leave it to Swindle."

Ben peered over his shoulder at the screen. "It says their sirens are one hundred and seventy-five decibels louder than revving jet engines. That means if we set it off, half the town will come running. Including the police — and my mother."

"Doesn't matter," Griffin told him. "We're not going to set it off. I wonder if his code is the same as the one at the store."

"That wouldn't help us," Ben pointed out. "Read this part — the e-alert feature. Every time the alarm is deactivated, the system automatically sends a message to your cell phone. So if we turn off his alarm, Swindle will be the first to know."

"And on top of it all, we've got Eli Mulroney, who came up out of the coal mine just to make our lives complicated," said Griffin. "He spends twenty-five hours a day staring at the very house we have to break into!"

"He doesn't seem to like Swindle any more than we do," Ben mused. "Maybe we should just explain what we're doing."

Griffin was horrified. "Are you crazy? I want your promise right now that you won't tell anybody — and I mean *nobody*!"

"We told Savannah," Ben reminded him. "And we'll still need her to get us past Luthor. Don't ask how that's going to happen. She hates our guts."

Griffin nodded slowly. "We could do with some help, and not just for the dog. But we can't know exactly who to recruit until we have a plan. And even having a plan seems pretty far away at this point."

"It better not be *too* far away. The auction is in eight days."

"We'll make it work," Griffin promised grimly. "It's more complicated than the store, but you tackle every problem one at a time. The neighbor, the dog, the alarm, the break-in, the safe —"

"The *what*?" Mr. Martinez appeared from behind a shelving cart. "The alarm, the break-in, the safe? Griffin! Ben! If I didn't know better, I'd swear you're planning a burglary!"

Griffin was appalled. On top of everything else they were facing, how could they be so careless as to spill the beans in front of their teacher? He looked at Ben and instantly knew there was going to be no assistance from that quarter. His best friend was paralyzed.

"You're right, Mr. Martinez," Griffin managed finally. "We *are* planning a burglary. At least Ben is."

Ben cast him a look of pure torment.

Griffin forged on. "For creative writing, Ben got this great idea to write about a big robbery. And in order to write it, you have to plan it like it's real."

Mr. Martinez broke into a delighted smile. "I think that's fantastic! What's being stolen, Ben?"

"Uh — a diamond necklace?" Ben croaked.

"That explains the safe," said the teacher. "How about the house you have to break into?"

"I haven't really figured it out yet," Ben offered faintly.

"That's part of the writer's craft," the teacher enthused. "You design the house to fit what you want to happen in the story. I have an idea. Go to the town hall. The building department has architectural drawings for every house in Cedarville. That should help your imagination take off."

It might not have helped Ben, but it did wonders for Griffin. If the building department had a floor plan for every house in town, that meant there would be one on file for 531 Park Avenue Extension. And seeing that layout might show them the way in.

14

Mrs. Annabelle Abernathy, the building department clerk at the Cedarville Town Hall, loved her files and treated them as if they were her children. So when two eleven-year-olds asked to see the original blueprints to 531 Park Avenue Extension, she was reluctant to hand them over.

"What do you want it for?" she asked dubiously.

"It's a project for school," Griffin replied, pleased that it was only half a lie, thanks to Mr. Martinez. "Town history, that kind of thing. Our job is to get a floor plan of a house built in the twenties or thirties."

"Well, all right," she said grudgingly. "But you have to go and wash your hands."

"Man, I am insulted," Ben complained as the two stood in the men's room, scrubbing. "Does she think we crawled here through the sewers?"

"It's the skate park thing all over again," Griffin muttered. "They treat kids like garbage in this place. If we can manage to photocopy those plans without drooling on them, she'll consider it a miracle. Just keep your cool. The last thing we need is for her to start asking too many questions."

Back at the desk, there was good news and bad news.

"I couldn't find 531 Park Avenue Extension," Mrs. Abernathy explained, "so I brought you the blueprints for 1414 Lakewood Road." She held up a cautionary finger when both boys opened their mouths to protest. "Hear me out. You're studying town history, and this is a part of it. Between 1925 and 1927, a builder named Gunhold put up six homes in Cedarville, all exactly alike. One was 531 Park Ex. Another is 1414 Lakewood. So this *is* the blueprint for the house you're asking about, since the plans are exactly the same."

Under Mrs. Abernathy's watchful eye, Griffin and Ben photocopied the drawings and left the town hall. Seconds later, the papers were spread out on a park bench as the boys tried to make sense of them.

"Who can read these things?" Griffin wondered aloud. "Where's the back door? Maybe we could get in that way, where Mr. Mulroney couldn't see us."

Ben squinted at the main floor layout. "I think it's a side door. There's nothing in the back. It's a solid line. Anyway, all the doors and windows will be covered by the alarm."

Griffin stared at the plans until he felt his eyes crossing. "If I ever say I want to become an architect, hit me with a shovel. I can't get a sense of the house from this. We're going to have to see the real thing."

"Oh, sure," Ben said sarcastically. "Swindle's going to invite us in for the grand tour."

"Probably not," Griffin agreed. "But the people at 1414 Lakewood might."

"Why would they?"

Griffin grinned. "Let's go over to Burger King and pick up some ketchup packets. I'll explain on the way."

When the lady of the house opened the door of 1414 Lakewood Road, the sight that met her eyes told a chilling story. Two boys stood on her front porch, the smaller of them dripping blood from a badly scraped arm.

As usual, Griffin did the talking. "My friend fell off his bike! Can we *please* come in and use the phone to call his mother?"

"Of course!" she exclaimed. "But first we need to wash that arm so it doesn't get infected! Come with me!"

"Thank you," whimpered Ben. He hoped she

attributed the weakness in his voice to shock rather than fear their hostess might clue in that the blood on his arm was really meant to be dolloped on French fries.

The woman hustled him up a flight of stairs and into a small white-tile bathroom.

"Wash your arm with soap," she instructed, rummaging in a drawer for antiseptic and bandages.

"I'll wait down here," Griffin called from below. He was already busily scouting the rooms and hallways, looking for an entry point from the outside. He felt a shiver of excitement as he looked around. Yes, he knew this wasn't really Swindle's house. Yet it was supposedly an exact replica. This was like being behind enemy lines. The heist was almost under way.

He unfolded the blueprint of the first floor, matching up walls and doorways. *Front door . . . side door . . . some of these windows would be big enough to crawl through . . .*

But what about the alarm?

Wait a minute — the basement!

He found the entrance and flitted silently down the cellar steps. The windowless basement was entirely underground, with no access to the outside. Another dead end.

In the second-story bathroom, Ben had finished washing the ketchup off his arm. It was a good thing he'd had that wipeout in front of the Bings' FOR SALE sign, he reflected. The scrapes were legitimate, even if the blood wasn't.

"See?" said the woman, spreading ointment on his skin. "It's already starting to scab over. You're a fast healer."

"Thanks," he mumbled. "Sorry to bother you." His mind was downstairs with Griffin. Had his friend made a breakthrough? Had he discovered a way into this house — Swindle's house, really — that wouldn't set off the alarm?

Suddenly the sun burst from behind a cloud, and a beam of light shot straight from the heavens to illuminate the white gauze that wrapped Ben's elbow.

Sunlight? But this bathroom had no windows!

Bewildered, he looked straight up, and there it was. The room was taller than it was wide, with a cathedral ceiling that followed the slope of the roof outside. Dead center was a heavy glass skylight.

"That's nice," he croaked, pointing skyward. "Is it a window, too? I mean, does it open?"

"It did," she replied. "We had a special pole to pop it up. But the pole broke years ago, and they don't make replacements anymore." She finished bandaging his arm. "Now let's go down and phone your mom."

"You know what? I don't want to scare her. I'll just ride home. I'm feeling a lot better."

And he was. But it had nothing to do with his arm.

He had found a way in.

15

Antonia "Pitch" Benson opened her locker and shrugged out of her backpack. She was in the process of stowing it on the shelf when the words jumped out at her: TOP SECRET.

At the base of the narrow space, sitting on her gym shoes, was a printed note on bright green paper, folded twice.

She opened it up and began to read:

> You have been chosen for your special skills to do something that urgently needs to be done. To learn more, come to the Ballroom at 3:30. Don't miss this. It will be worth your while—$$$.

"What's that?"

She wheeled around to see Darren Vader craning his neck to read over her shoulder. "Mind your own business!" she barked angrily, snapping the note out of his view. She refolded the paper and pocketed it.

Now what could that be about? Someone had obviously slipped it through the vents in her locker door. But who? And why her? Her only talent was rock-climbing, and there weren't any mountains or crags near Cedarville.

The whole thing was probably just a joke. And if Darren was behind it, she would be expressing her displeasure with her fists.

She slammed her locker shut. Whatever it was, she'd know at 3:30.

"Dad, this athlete's foot itch is driving me crazy! Isn't there anything we can do?"

Logan Kellerman had never been so well pre-pared for an audition. He had rehearsed his line so many times that he knew it inside out. He understood every subtle shade of it, especially his character's motivation. He was someone who didn't want to be itchy anymore, and who knew his father loved him enough to buy an exciting new product to make him feel better. The role had become so much a part of him that sometimes he could actually feel the prickling irritation between his toes. There was no way the director of that commercial could overlook his performance. No way in the world.

"Dad, this athlete's foot itch —" He was halfway through the speech again when he noticed the green piece of paper at the bottom of his locker.

You have been chosen for your special skills . . .

Special skills. Logan's heart beat faster. This could only be about some kind of acting job!

The Ballroom at 3:30. He could hardly wait!

*　　*　　*

Melissa Dukakis wasn't sure what to make of the folded green invitation. She had never been invited to anything before. *Special skills*. What could that mean? She was a C student who didn't know a lot of people and kept to herself.

Maybe this was a mistake — the wrong locker, or maybe the wrong Melissa. There were several others in the school. That must be it. A mistake.

She would go at 3:30 — just to explain the mix-up.

The green TOP SECRET note crumpled in her pocket, Savannah Drysdale stormed past the gym. She'd been halfway home before she'd changed her mind about this meeting. Why lose sleep wondering what all the secrecy was about — as if she didn't already know. Griffin Bing and his sawed-off sidekick.

The Ballroom was actually a storage area by the gym. It was piled high with dead tennis balls, shattered Ping-Pong balls, ripped baseballs, cracked golf balls, squashed soccer balls, leaky footballs and basketballs, lopsided medicine balls, untethered tether balls, and balls from sports that no one ever played — bocce balls, water polo balls, rugger balls, and even a few that no one could identify.

Coach Nimitz could not bring himself to throw away a ball, and truly believed that one day he would find the right pump or patch. Then all this equipment could be used to promote physical fitness for children.

It was in this rubber and horsehide graveyard that Savannah found the meeting already in progress. Along with Griffin and Ben, she was surprised to see Pitch, Logan, and Melissa lounging on the soft piles of Phys Ed castoffs.

"You two!" Savannah spat. "I knew it! This is about your stupid baseball card, isn't it?"

"You were right to be angry before," Griffin told her seriously. "We should have been honest with you from the very beginning. We won't make that mistake again."

Pitch was bewildered. "What baseball card?"

"Before we go any further," Griffin said solemnly, "I need your word that what's said in this room stays in this room. In or out, you can't tell anybody about this. Ever. This is no kids' game. There's serious stuff on the line — serious money, but also serious trouble if anything goes wrong. If you don't think you can handle it, there's the door."

Nobody moved, not even Savannah, who knew what was coming.

Pitch spoke up. "All right, Griffin, you've got our attention. What's this about?"

"A Babe Ruth card from 1920 — the kind collectors pay big bucks for." Griffin gave them the whole story, from the discovery in the old Rockford house to Swindle's deceitful flimflam and the unsuccessful break-in at the store.

"So it's about the money, but not *just* the money," he concluded. "Swindle saw a couple of kids, and he took advantage of us because he didn't think we could do anything about it. We're going to show him he was wrong."

Logan cleared his throat. "How much money are we talking about?"

"Equal shares, split six ways," Griffin replied. "We can't know the total amount, because it's being sold at an auction. But the rock-bottom starting bid is two hundred thousand dollars. And Swindle told the TV news he thought it could go for over a million."

"A million dollars!" Melissa performed the calculation at lightning speed in her head. "That's one hundred sixty-six thousand six hundred sixty-six each! I could buy a state-of-the-art computer."

"And build a new wing on your house to keep it in," Ben added.

"I could afford acting lessons from Sanjay Jotwani," said Logan dreamily.

"I could take my family climbing at Yosemite," exclaimed Pitch in awe.

Savannah was not as easily impressed. "Yeah, yeah, it's a lot of money. I'd love to grow up knowing I've got enough in the bank to pay my way through veterinary school. Who wouldn't? But that kind of cash doesn't come easy. You're talking about a robbery, not a Sunday picnic."

"You're right," said Griffin. "Still, if we all work together, we can pull it off. We break into Swindle's house through a skylight on the roof. Pitch, that's where you come in. Your job is to get us there."

"Like climbing on a building instead of a mountain," she mused.

"The house has an alarm system, but the motion sensors will be off. We know this because Swindle has a guard dog that sleeps in the house. The dog's no joke, but Savannah can handle him."

"Deep down, he's a real sweetheart," Savannah said fondly.

Melissa shook her head, clearing the veil of hair away from her face. "So my role is to get to the panel and disarm the alarm?"

Pitch regarded her in amazement. "You can do that?"

Ben shook his head. "Doesn't matter. That's the last thing we want to do. If anyone shuts down the system, Swindle gets notified by e-alert."

Melissa frowned. "So what do you need me for?"

"You know more about computers than anybody else in this town," Griffin replied. "Can you hack into Swindle's e-mail?"

"Probably. But what for?"

"We need to find a time when he's going to be out of the house for a few hours. We can't have him busting in on us when we're stealing our card back."

Logan was confused. "Where do I fit into all this? I'm an actor, not a burglar."

"Swindle lives across the street from the great-granddaddy of all nosy neighbors,"

Griffin replied. "His name is Eli Mulroney, and he has the whole block under surveillance twenty-four/seven. His chair is pointed right at Swindle's front door. We need you to focus your acting skills on making friends with this guy so you can distract him during the operation. And you'll be a lookout at the same time."

Griffin got up from the flattened exercise ball he'd been using as a beanbag chair. "I know it sounds crazy. And I know it sounds dangerous. But if you break it down into everybody doing their job, you'll see that no single part is impossible. We just have to put all the pieces together in the right order. We can do this! Now, who's on board?"

16

The silence was earsplitting.

Finally, Pitch spoke up. "Count me in. Somebody's got to teach this creep a lesson."

Logan was next. "Me, too. It's the ultimate challenge for an actor."

"Easy for you to say," muttered Savannah. "You'll be safe and sound across the street. If the cops come, you can tell them you've never seen us before in your life."

"It may be a break-in, but it isn't stealing," Griffin reminded them. "That card is *ours*. If any stealing happened, it was Swindle who did it."

"Sure," Savannah said sarcastically. "That's the first thing that pops into a policeman's mind when he catches you blowtorching a safe."

"If you don't make the payments on your car," Griffin argued, "they send a guy to repossess it. He steals it just like any car thief would, but it's perfectly legal. That's exactly what we're doing — repossessing a baseball card."

Melissa spoke up. "I thought that note was in my locker by mistake. But I guess you guys really did want me."

"Of course we did," Ben assured her. "But are you in or out?"

"Oh, I'm in," she confirmed. "It's the first time anybody's ever asked me to do anything."

Savannah was the picture of outrage. "I would have bet *five* of those Babe Ruth cards that you guys were going to stand up and tell these two maniacs to stuff it. What's the matter with you people?"

Griffin regarded her intently. "It all comes down to you, Savannah."

"Yeah, right — like I've got a choice," she raged. "You've fixed it so I *have* to go along, just to protect poor Luthor!"

Ben couldn't believe his ears. "Poor Luthor?"

"I can picture exactly how it'll play out. You're going to bumble around that house until he's got no choice but to bite one of you. Then the ASPCA is going to want to put him down because he's vicious. Well, he's not! That's why I'm going to be there every step of the way — to make sure nothing happens to Luthor."

"It's a go, then," Griffin announced. "The auction is on October seventeenth. That gives us five days to make our move. I don't have to tell you that total secrecy is a must. You can't talk to *anybody* about this, no matter how good you think they are at keeping secrets. No best friends, no favorite grandmothers, no personal life coaches, not even your pen pal who lives in Hong Kong. *No one else* can find out about this!"

On that note, a pile of flattened volleyballs sneezed.

"Bless you," Ben said automatically. Then, "Hey —"

Balls began tumbling in all directions as the mountain moved. A head broke the surface of the rockslide as Darren Vader got to his feet.

"How much did you hear?" Griffin demanded.

"All of it," Darren replied cheerfully. "That's quite a plan you've got there, Bing. When the funeral home starts burying people in Ziploc bags, I'll know some of you fell off the roof."

"If you breathe a word of this —"

"Take it easy, shorty," Darren interrupted. "I don't want to rat you out. I want a piece of the action."

"What are you talking about?" Griffin snapped. "A piece of what action?"

"I want in on the heist."

"No way," Griffin ruled. "We picked the team to fit the plan. If we suddenly have an opening for an obnoxious bigmouth, you'll be the first person we call."

"You need me," Darren argued. "You've got a climber, an actor, a computer geek, and a dog handler. But you're missing one thing — muscle."

"A baseball card isn't very heavy," Ben said evenly.

"But people are — especially if you have to lower them by ropes, or pull them up again. Through a skylight, let's say."

"I don't care how strong you are," Griffin seethed. "You don't call the shots. There are six of us and only one of you."

"Fine. But if I have to walk out of here, I'm going straight to Mr. Palomino."

Griffin stared at him, his eyes twin lasers. "You wouldn't dare!"

Darren seemed surprised. "It wouldn't take much daring from me. *You're* the ones who are going to get into a ton of trouble."

Griffin read Darren's mocking expression and knew that the threat was very real. Darren had been his nemesis since kindergarten. He wouldn't hesitate to sell them out.

It had all come down to either/or. Either let Darren in or give up the plan altogether.

He looked from face to face at Ben and the team. One at a time, they nodded.

Pitch was last. "It can't hurt to have a muscle-head around."

Darren beamed. "You won't regret this."

Griffin regretted it already.

17

The next day, Logan Kellerman started up the walk at 530 Park Avenue Extension, a package under his arm.

Eli Mulroney was sitting on his porch, just as Griffin and Ben had been certain he'd be. *"He's always there,"* Griffin had said. *"We passed by that place a dozen different times. He might as well be a pink flamingo on the lawn."*

"What can I do for you, son?"

Logan beamed at the old man. "I live at 530 University, and this parcel was delivered to our house by mistake. Are you" — he consulted the label — "E. Mulroney?"

"That's my name. But I'm not expecting any packages."

Logan stepped onto the porch and showed the old man the label — fresh from the printer of Melissa's computer.

Mr. Mulroney looked bewildered. "That's me, all right. Who's it from?"

Logan shrugged. "It doesn't say. Maybe there's a card inside."

The old man produced a lethal-looking pocketknife and neatly slit the taped sides of the carton. Several hundred Styrofoam peanuts scattered across the porch.

"God bless America!" he roared at the mess. Then he pulled out a magnetic chess, checkers, and backgammon set, a box of dominoes, a deck of cards, and a Monopoly game.

"No note?" asked Logan.

"I'm not reaching in there! Those fool peanuts stick to your hand and you can't shake them off!"

"Well, it must be from someone who knows you like games," Logan persisted.

"I hate games!" Mulroney snapped. "Although" — his eyes gleamed — "I used to be a real whiz at backgammon. Of course, that was a long time ago."

Logan sensed the opening and went for it. "I always wanted to play backgammon. Would you teach me? You know, if you have time?"

The old man raised an eyebrow. "Doesn't a kid like you have something better to do than pal around with an old geezer?"

This is it! thought Logan. Time for his talent to shine. He cultivated a wan look that was part shy and part sad.

"Not really. We just moved here. I haven't made any friends yet."

"Pull up a chair, son. What's your name?"

Logan's heart was pounding. His first real acting job. And this one could bring in the biggest paycheck this side of Hollywood.

That night, the heist team gathered in the Bings' garage for the unveiling of Griffin's new plan. The SmartPick leaned against the wall, standing like a sentry over the crowded workbench, the nerve center of the operation.

THE GREAT BASEBALL CARD HEIST —
ROUND TWO

The Team:

(i) GRIFFIN BING: Team leader and blowtorch operator

(ii) BEN SLOVAK: Lieutenant and tight spaces specialist

(iii) SAVANNAH DRYSDALE: Dog whisperer

(iv) LOGAN KELLERMAN: Nosy neighbor neutralizer and lookout #1

(v) ANTONIA "PITCH" BENSON: Second-story woman

(vi) MELISSA DUKAKIS: Electronics and lookout #2

(vii) DARREN VADER: Muscle and miscellaneous

Rendezvous Point: Water Tower
Entry Point: Skylight

"Okay" — Griffin turned to Pitch — "how do we get in?"

"We're going to need a twenty-four-foot extension ladder," she replied. "That'll get us to the edge of the roof." She produced a photograph of the rear of the Palomino house. "See that vent pipe? We'll loop a rope around it. Then we can climb up and over to the skylight, which is right here" — she pointed — "just below the peak on the east side."

"Sounds simple enough," said Griffin.

"If you're a mountain goat," Ben added nervously.

"It's not as scary as you think," Pitch assured him. "We'll wear climbing harnesses up on the roof. Even if you fall, you don't fall. I'll run you guys through a quick Mountaineering 101 before we go. But that's just to get you used to the equipment. There's no real danger."

"Right," Griffin approved. "Okay, Logan, you're next. How's it going with Mr. Mulroney?"

Logan was his usual modest self. "If they gave Academy Awards for heists, I'd walk

137

away with all the hardware. I have cre-
ated a role so real, so three-dimensional, so
heartwarming —"

"Just spit it out!" Darren demanded
impatiently.

"He's teaching me to play backgammon.
But it's so much more. I've truly *become* this
character."

"I should hope so," said Griffin. "It's *you*!
You're playing yourself! And the whole point is
to make sure the old guy doesn't get a whiff of
what we're doing and call the cops. Now what's
your report?"

"Nothing gets Mr. Mulroney out of the chair,
that's for sure," Logan told them. "He takes
bathroom breaks, he makes sandwiches to eat
outside. He says he only needs three or four
hours of sleep a night. He's kind of a wing nut,
and you know what? I like him a lot. Maybe I'm
a wing nut, too."

"You think?" put in Darren in a voice that
dripped with sarcasm.

"Oh, yeah," added Logan. "He's really proud of the fact that even at his age, he still has twenty-twenty vision."

Ben held his head. "You sure there isn't anything else we need to know? Maybe his rocking chair has radar?"

"No, that's pretty much it. Except the skylight. You can see it from Mr. Mulroney's porch, even at night. The streetlight reflects off the glass."

Ben blew his stack. "When were you planning on mentioning this? When the guy's dialing nine-one-one on heist night?"

"We'll have to figure out a way to turn off the streetlight for a while," said Griffin. "Now, Melissa, have you made any progress hacking into Swindle's e-mail?"

Melissa parted her hair. "Oh, that's already done. He has two addresses, one personal and one for business. They both run through the Web site he set up for his store. Every message he gets comes to my computer first."

"What we need," Griffin explained, "is a time when it's safe to make our move. You know, a good three- or four-hour window when he'll definitely be out of the house."

"I didn't see anything like that."

"How about a weekend out of town?" Ben persisted. "A wedding or a family reunion? Even a big fancy dinner in New York City?"

She shrugged. "Not really. Most of his personal e-mail is just spam. There was something from the New York Rangers Booster Club and a notice from E-Grocer that his twenty-pound turkey had been shipped."

Griffin was disgusted. "Oh, sure! Like a nasty, obnoxious crook knows enough people willing to sit down and eat a twenty-pound turkey with him!"

"Well," Logan reasoned, "Thanksgiving isn't too far away."

"If you've got nothing better to do on a holiday than hang out with Swindle," Ben said sadly, "you've got nothing to be thankful for."

"This is just peachy." Griffin moaned. "We've got the perfect plan and no chance to try it, because we can't get that jerk out of the house."

"Could we try it during the day, when he's at the store?" Savannah suggested.

"I thought of that," said Griffin. "It's just too exposed. The ladder alone would stand out like a sore thumb."

Darren laughed out loud. "Bing, you're such a dope! This auction is going to come and go while you sit around waiting for him to go to the movies. Use your brain. If you want him out, get him out!"

Pitch was angry. "We can't kidnap the guy!"

"He sells sports memorabilia," Darren ranted. "He's a Rangers fan. Buy him a ticket to a hockey game."

"Oh, yeah!" Griffin seethed. " 'Here's a little thank-you gift for ripping us off.' That'll work!"

"Maybe we could mail it to him with a letter saying he won it as a prize," Savannah suggested.

Griffin shook his head. "He'd see through it in a second. You don't win a contest when you never entered one."

Darren was growing exasperated. "Here's what you do: Stick the ticket in a birthday card with somebody else's name on the envelope, and drop it in Swindle's mail slot like somebody delivered it to the wrong house. If this guy is as rotten as you say he is, he won't be able to resist the idea that he's cheating somebody out of a ticket. Of course he'll go to the game. And he'll stay to the last shot of the final period."

"Is that how your sick mind works?" Pitch asked, revolted.

"No!" Griffin said excitedly. "I think Darren's onto something!"

Griffin Bing and Darren Vader had never been friends. Griffin had accepted Darren on the team only because he'd been blackmailed into it. He disliked Darren, but even worse, he didn't trust him. And in an operation like this, trust was everything.

But now he was coming to understand that Darren brought a talent to the heist that even the boy himself didn't see.

Darren was so awful that he was actually capable of thinking like Swindle.

18

HEIST DAY: Thursday, October 16

HOCKEY GAME: Madison Square Garden —
Rangers vs. Maple Leafs — PUCK DROPS @ 8 p.m.

Swindle LEAVES for NYC: 6:30-7:00

SUNDOWN: 6:41

ZERO HOUR: 7:30

Griffin sat back and examined the time table. It should all go like clockwork. They had the right plan and the right people. They should be able to nab the card and be safe at home before the start of the third period of the Rangers game — even allowing for the odd glitch.

He wasn't totally comfortable with the idea of the heist taking place the very day before Worthington's Annual Sports Memorabilia Auction. But there was no way around it. The Rangers were coming off a long road trip, and Thursday was their only game in New York before the seventeenth. It was the sixteenth or never. And never was not an option.

He regarded the single hockey ticket that sat on his desk. Eighty bucks for a jerk like Swindle! His one consolation was that he and Ben had paid for the ticket out of the money that crook had given them for the Babe Ruth card. There was a kind of poetry to it — - Swindle financing his own downfall with his sleazy dealings.

Revenge was going to be sweet.

Still, Griffin couldn't shake an uneasy feeling. Everyone was risking serious trouble by being a part of this. If something went wrong on

Thursday, and they were caught, Griffin knew he would have to find a way to take all the blame. This was *his* struggle, *his* family's fate. Ben and the others shouldn't have to pay for that.

Okay, I admit it. I'm nervous. A little dose of fear is good in an operation like this. It keeps you sharp.

He hit a key on his computer to bring the monitor out of screen-saver mode. Sure enough, there was another message from Melissa. Subject: HOMEWORK, their code word for heist business. Melissa had been sending him copies of Swindle's intercepted e-mails.

This one was a video clip advertising Worthington's Annual Sports Memorabilia Auction. Griffin clicked on the link and watched a sixty-second promo video, his lip curling with outrage. The Babe Ruth card was the talk of this year's event. The announcer called it "the most exciting find in the past half-century." There was an excerpt from an interview with S. Wendell Palomino. It showed the smirking creep looking on while a

146

conference table of experts oohed and aahed over the Bambino. One of them even compared it to the famous Honus Wagner card. Everyone agreed it was going to sell for a fortune.

"Magnificent!" pronounced a man who was holding the treasure under a magnifying glass. "But why is it so cold?"

The self-satisfied con man had an answer, like he always did: "That's for all the cold hard cash it's going to bring in!"

By the time it was over, Griffin was shaking with fury. Whatever doubts he might have had about Thursday night disappeared at the sound of Swindle's smug gloating. This flim-flam artist could not be allowed to profit from his crime.

Sometimes it took an act of thievery to stop a thief.

The sun was setting as S. Wendell Palomino unlocked his door, stepped into the foyer, and keyed in the code that turned off his alarm.

He was in a good mood. It was easy to be in a good mood when you were rich — or at least when you would be on Friday.

He bent over and picked up the mail that had been dropped through the slot.

Bill . . . bill . . . magazine . . . junk mail — what was this?

The blue square envelope had no address or stamp, which meant that someone had delivered it by hand. And to the wrong house, because the notation on the front said: *To Uncle Archie With Love.*

Without a qualm, he ripped the envelope open and pulled out a brightly colored birthday card. Inside was written: *Happy 50th. Enjoy the game! Love, Maggie and Ted.*

A ticket to Thursday night's Rangers–Leafs game was attached by a paper clip.

A slow smile spread over Palomino's broad face. *Better and better,* he reflected, sunny-side-up eyes gleaming.

Well, maybe not for Archie. He's not going to the game. I am.

19

Thursday — the day of the operation.

Griffin could not remember school time so utterly wasted. Mr. Martinez might as well have been delivering his lessons in Swahili for all that Griffin was listening. His mind was lost in the details of the plan. It was like being scheduled to wrestle an alligator later, but right now you were expected to alphabetize spelling words and pretend it was important.

He could tell the other team members were also feeling the pressure. When Ben went down to the nurse for his allergy medication, he tripped over his own feet on the way out. Pitch was focused and distant. Logan was mumbling to himself more than usual, and his ramblings had nothing to do with upcoming auditions. Savannah was so distracted that she was halfway through her sandwich before remembering to ask the cafeteria ladies if it had been made using dolphin-safe tuna. Even Darren was quiet, withdrawn, and slightly less obnoxious than usual.

As for Melissa, nobody could tell. She might have been freaking out behind that curtain of hair. One thing was sure — she was still on the job, toting her laptop around, monitoring Swindle's e-mail.

It was after lunch, Zero Hour minus six, when she approached Griffin. "We have a problem," she whispered.

Griffin tried not to let his trepidation show as he looked at the message on the screen.

Mr. Palomino:
Due to increased media attention, Worthington Auction
House has decided to pick up your item on Thursday

afternoon, rather than Friday morning. Our bonded courier
will be at your house between 4:30 and 5:00 p.m.
Please reconfirm your address: 531 Park Avenue
Extension, Cedarville, New York.
Yours truly,
Eric Mansfield, Courier Dispatch

All Griffin's panic came out through Ben's mouth. "That's two hours *before* we move in!" the smaller boy cried. "Griffin, what are we going to do? We can't steal a card that's already in New York City!"

Griffin was practicing deep breathing, struggling to keep control. "Okay — I'm glad this happened. This is good news."

Ben was appalled. "How do you figure that?"

"Something unexpected happens in *every* plan. Now we've got that out of the way, and we can work around it."

"The card not being there anymore isn't something we can work around!" Ben rasped.

"Swindle hasn't seen this message yet," Melissa reminded them. "I stopped it before it ever got to his computer. Couldn't we just answer the auction guy and pretend to be Swindle? We could tell him to come a few hours later."

"Too risky," said Griffin, whistling between his teeth. "If they can't do it, they might try to phone. What would be perfect is if they just got lost."

"Maybe we could give them the wrong directions," Ben suggested.

"They're not asking for directions," Melissa pointed out. "They've probably got one of those satellite navigation systems."

Griffin's thoughtful expression bloomed into a wide grin. "Let me see that computer." He swiveled the laptop around and began to type:

Mr. Mansfield — URGENT! Note address correction.

The town is not Cedarville. It is CEDAR SPRINGS.

Thanks.

S. Wendell Palomino

The three exchanged nervous smiles. Cedar Springs was in Westchester County, sixty miles away.

At 6:30 — Zero Hour minus one — Logan Kellerman rode his bike down Park Avenue Extension and pulled onto the driveway of number 530.

Eli Mulroney was already in his usual spot on the front porch. The only difference in the retired miner's unbreakable routine was that there were now two rockers out there, separated by a low table that held the backgammon board.

"I'm surprised you've got the guts to show your face around here," the old man taunted, "after how badly I kicked you around last time."

Logan smiled. "It's only eleven games to seven." Losing, but not too obviously, was all part of the acting job. This role would be for

Logan what *Pirates of the Caribbean* was for Johnny Depp.

They set up the pieces, anchoring the board with a stone as protection against the stiff breeze.

"Windy tonight," Logan commented. "I wasn't sure you'd be out."

Mulroney cackled. "We're catching the northern edge of that big storm pounding the Carolinas. Gusts up to fifty miles per hour." He rolled the dice.

Logan looked across the street to the steep roof of Swindle's house and shuddered.

They began to play, with Mr. Mulroney jumping to an early advantage. Neither took much notice of the three girls who were Rollerblading on the sidewalk.

Logan, of course, knew they were Melissa, Savannah, and Pitch. Nor was he surprised when all three chose the patch of grass around the streetlight to sit down and tighten their skate laces. Furthermore, he understood that only two of them were attending to laces.

Melissa, hidden by the others, was unscrewing the access panel at the base of the pole.

She slipped on an insulated glove, reached in with a tiny wire cutter and snipped every electrical cable she could find. Then she replaced the faceplate, and the three girls bladed off along the street. The entire procedure was over in less time than it took Mr. Mulroney to decide how to play his double fives.

The door of number 531 opened and Swindle stepped out, dressed in a voluminous New York Rangers jersey that covered his ample stomach and stretched almost to his knees. He got into his Honda Element and drove off in the direction of the highway.

Griffin would be pleased. Swindle had taken the bait. Everything was setting up nicely for the operation tonight.

A few minutes later, when the streetlights came on, the one in front of the Palomino home remained dark.

20

When night fell, six dark-clad figures, wearing gloves and stocking caps, met in the grass beneath the huge tank of the Cedarville municipal water tower. The wind plucked at their clothing and howled through the support girders all around them.

Griffin thought he could never be happy to see the nasty leering face of Darren Vader. But Darren looked pretty good to him tonight, especially since the big boy was lugging his father's giant folding aluminum ladder. Griffin peered around, counting heads. The team was in place.

He shrugged his shoulders to resettle the blowtorch strapped to his back. He cleared his throat and launched into the speech he'd been preparing in his head ever since the idea for this heist had been hatched.

"What we're doing tonight isn't about a baseball card," he began. "It isn't even about money. Tonight we show that fairness isn't something that's just for adults, and that you can't get away with dumping on people just because they're younger than you. Tonight we make our statement. Tonight —"

"Yada, yada, yada," drawled Darren in a bored voice. "Can it, Bing. I'm not in the mood."

"As much as I hate to agree with Darren," Pitch added, "he's right. We're all scared enough, Griffin. We don't need to talk about *why* we're doing this. Let's just do it."

Griffin nodded, hiding his disappointment. "Okay, let's go."

As dog whisperer, Savannah was the first over the fence. She called for Luthor a few times, then stood silently, almost as if she were trying to sense the animal's presence. "He's not outside," she finally reported.

One by one they crossed the fence. Darren was last, handing the ladder over to Griffin before clambering up and jumping to Swindle's lawn.

It was when they got to the rear of the house, as Darren and Pitch were unfolding the four six-foot sections, that Griffin felt a tug at his sleeve. Ben.

"Griffin, I've got to talk to you."

"Can it wait?"

Ben grabbed his friend tightly by the arm. "I can't go on the roof."

Griffin was thunderstruck. "Of course you can!"

"No, I can't. I thought I could, but I can't. I'm sorry."

Griffin pulled his friend aside. "I was worried about one of these clowns wimping out the way they did the night of the old Rockford house, but *you*? What are you afraid of? The wind? We'll be harnessed, remember?"

"I'm afraid I'll fall asleep," Ben said in a sheepish voice.

Griffin was beside himself. "Fall asleep? Are we *boring* you? The heist isn't exciting enough to keep you awake? What more do you need? Air-raid sirens?"

"Don't make jokes! I never told anybody about this. I have narcolepsy."

"What? What's that?"

"My body has trouble regulating sleep," Ben explained. "I might fall into a deep sleep any time of the day or night."

"But that doesn't happen to you," Griffin protested. "Does it?"

"You can control it by taking short naps during the day," Ben explained. He flushed. "You know how I go to the nurse for allergy medicine? Well, it's not allergies. I take a fifteen-minute nap, and it gets me through the afternoon. But whenever my schedule is off, my narcolepsy gets worse. Remember when I fell asleep inside the crate in Swindle's store?"

Griffin was chastened. "I'm really sorry, man. I had no clue."

"I thought I could tough it through," Ben went on miserably, "but I'm yawning, my eyelids are heavy, I'm feeling all the signs. I don't want to leave you in the lurch, but there are no do-overs for falling off a ladder. Not to mention that I could wipe out the whole team on the way down."

Griffin made a split-second decision. "Guys," he announced, "change of plan. Ben's going to take the lookout spot in the front bushes. Melissa, that means you have to go in from the roof with us. Are you up for it?"

Melissa parted her hair, and even in the darkness, it was obvious that her eyes were gleaming. She handed her walkie-talkie to Ben. "Good luck."

"Good luck to all of us," said Pitch, unzipping her duffel bag. Five climbing harnesses tumbled out. As Ben set off around the side of the house, slinking through the shadows, Pitch fitted her teammates into their vests.

There was a soft thud as the extended ladder touched into place against the side of the house. The break-in had begun.

With Pitch in the lead, the team made the climb in close order. Twenty-four feet had never felt so far or so high. The wind seemed to be trying to tear them free of the aluminum rungs. Only Pitch's calm encouragement kept them moving upward — that and the fact that retreat was just as unthinkable.

Griffin was in second position, right behind Pitch. He'd heard a lot about her family and their climbing skills, but this was the first time he'd witnessed them in real life. Her work was impressive. Anchored by nothing more than the strength and sureness of her hands and feet, she ascended the steep grade toward the high peak of the roof. There, hanging on by the sheer tension in her body, she pulled the coil of rope from her shoulder, lashed one end to a steel vent pipe, and ran the other end through the clip on her harness.

Now securely tethered, she strung four more cords around the pipe and carried these back down to her novice climbers on the ladder. One by one, she threaded the ropes through their vests and hauled them up to the roof.

Even knowing they were safely harnessed was barely enough to keep Griffin from depositing his dinner on Swindle's black shingles. The environment was so alien that he felt like he was attempting a space walk — the unfamiliar slant of the surface under him, the buffeting wind, the near-total darkness.

In painful silence, the team crawled up to the peak and over. Now they were descending the front of the roof, inching toward the skylight that was their way in.

Suddenly, Darren was sliding out of control down the incline. He didn't scream, but Griffin caught a glimpse of eyes wide with horror as the boy slipped helplessly past the skylight, heading for a twenty-foot drop.

Barely a yard from the edge, his rope went taut, and he was no longer moving. Pitch was as good as her word: *Even if you fall, you don't fall.*

"Relax," she called softly. "Catch your breath and meet us at the skylight."

Darren nodded, chastened. It was one of the rare occasions when he had no smart-aleck comment to offer. He got to his knees, advancing along his rope, hand over hand.

A few minutes later, the five members of the heist team were assembled around the skylight.

Griffin and Pitch felt around the gasket that water-sealed the pyramid-shaped window. Their fingers fit easily underneath the rubber, and they were able to pry the heavy glass up.

Triumph surged through Griffin as he looked down into Swindle's second-story bathroom. They were in.

21

In all the years he had worked as a bonded courier for the Worthington Auction House, Lamar Fontaine had never been so lost. Cedar Springs, New York, was a tiny hamlet tucked in a remote corner of Westchester County. There was a Park Avenue, but no Park Avenue Extension. If you extended Park Avenue, you'd end up at the bottom of a lake. And there was definitely no number 531. There weren't 531 houses in the whole town, and probably not 531 Cedar Springers.

He felt like he'd already spoken to most of them, asking directions. This was worse than the time he'd had to transport that Ming vase through Brooklyn during the big blackout.

He finally located a gas station and went inside for help. The mini-mart clerk had no idea, but one of the customers was able to shed some light on the subject.

"Listen, I don't want to tell you your business, but I grew up on Long Island, and I think what you're looking for is Cedarville, not Cedar Springs. They've got the only Park Avenue Extension I know."

"Thanks." Fontaine returned to his SUV. Wrong town. Wrong county. Wrong part of the state. It was the Ming vase all over again. Why him?

Five nylon ropes slapped to the floor of the bathroom under the skylight.

Savannah lowered herself first, eyes peeled for signs of Luthor. "All clear," she called up.

Griffin descended next, followed by Melissa and then Darren, who left a trail of boot marks on the wall. Griffin handed him a towel to erase the evidence.

Pitch made sure the others were safely inside before jumping on her own rope and starting down. All at once, there was a screech of tearing metal, and she was plummeting toward them. Griffin moved to try to cushion her fall. Between himself and Darren, they half-caught her, but could not prevent her ankle from twisting as it hit the tile floor.

"Ow!"

The broken vent pipe came next, jagged and rusty, bearing all five climbing ropes.

"Pitch, are you all right?" Griffin hissed urgently.

Gritting her teeth, Pitch tested her right leg. She winced in pain. "I don't think it's broken," she managed, "but it's a nasty sprain!"

"Can you walk?" asked Savannah.

"I'll manage," Pitch replied stoically. "But I won't be doing any climbing." She looked ruefully at the piece of pipe and its tangle of nylon. "I guess none of us will be."

The awful truth dawned on Griffin. "Are you saying that we're trapped in here?"

Pitch nodded sadly. "I could have gotten up there myself and rigged something for the rest of you guys. But not now."

Griffin reached for the walkie-talkie on his belt. "Ben, we've got a situation here. You've got to find a way to get up that ladder and drop us a new rope. I know it's not something you want to do, but this is an emergency. Pitch is —" He frowned. "Ben! Ben, are you there?" He slapped the handset against his thigh. "Come in, Ben! Please!"

He looked at the others. "Ben's out of the picture for a while. It's a long story."

"Are you saying," Savannah asked in horror, "that we've got no choice but to wait around here until Swindle comes home and finds us?"

"Forget that," Darren said flatly. "Worse comes to worst, we walk out the front door.

So the alarm goes off — big deal. I'll take my chances beating the cops home."

"No alarm!" Griffin exclaimed. "Nobody opens a door or a window unless I say so. We stick to the plan."

Darren indicated the injured Pitch. "Your precious plan is busted, or haven't you noticed?"

"The plan is finding the card first," Griffin insisted. "Then we worry about getting out."

Melissa emerged from her hair. "I'll check the alarm box in the meantime. There might be something I can do."

"You can't shut down the system," Griffin warned. "That'll contact Swindle, and he'll call the police for sure."

"I'll be careful," Melissa promised. "Trust me."

Griffin was amazed at how much he actually *did* trust her. "Everybody — remember to keep your gloves on. No fingerprints." He swallowed hard. Maybe this operation wasn't doomed yet.

His thoughts were interrupted by a long low growl from out in the hall. When Luthor's black and tan head hove into view in Griffin's flashlight beam, the Doberman was already moving at full speed in attack mode.

"Savannah!" Griffin squeaked, pushing the dog whisperer into the path of ninety pounds of raw canine power.

Savannah pulled off her stocking cap, allowing her long hair to spill onto her shoulders. "Luthor! *Sweetie!*"

The big guard dog interrupted itself in mid-pounce, landing on its back, wriggling like a puppy and presenting its belly to be scratched.

Savannah obliged, cooing, "Good boy — beautiful boy! Oh, I missed you so much!"

"Okay, guys." It wasn't until Griffin let out his breath that he realized he'd been holding it. "Split up. We have to find that safe."

*　　*　　*

Pitch limped into a small guest bedroom and sat down hard on the bed. She pulled up the leg of her jeans and shined her flashlight on her ankle. It didn't look too bad yet, but she knew that if she dared to take off her shoe, she'd never be able to get it back on again. This was going to swell up like a watermelon. She should probably be icing it right now. But in the middle of a heist, who had time? No way was she going to let the others down any more than she already had by getting hurt.

Griffin came in. "Any sign of the safe?"

Pitch hobbled over and checked the small closet. "Nothing."

Griffin noticed the grimace that accompanied her every step. "Are you going to be okay? Maybe you should sit this out. We'll find it."

"I'll live," Pitch assured him.

"Make sure you do." He ran out into the dark hall, where he nearly bumped into Savannah and the dog.

"Griffin, there's something wrong with Luthor."

"Yeah, he's a psychopath. What else is new?"

"I'm serious! He's nervous and upset. He keeps looking over his shoulder. I think he's trying to tell me something." As if to prove her point, the dog closed its teeth gently on her sleeve and began tugging her toward the stairs. "See?"

"Look," Griffin said impatiently, "we'll make an anonymous phone call tomorrow and tell Swindle to take him to the vet. But right now you're just going to have to wing it. As long as the dog isn't chewing on anybody, he's fine. Okay?"

"But, Griffin —"

All at once, Darren's voice called, "I've got it! It's here!"

22

The searchers converged on the master bedroom. Darren was on his hands and knees, aiming his flashlight under the nightstand. There, half hidden and bolted to the floor, stood the safe Griffin had first seen behind the counter in Palomino's Emporium of Collectibles and Memorabilia.

The safe that held the million-dollar prize.

Griffin pulled the blowtorch off his back and produced safety goggles and a flint lighter from his pocket.

"Give me some space, you guys," he said.

He turned on the gas and sparked the flint to ignite the flame.

*   *   *

Melissa had been staring at the front entrance for at least twenty minutes. The more she thought about it, the more obvious the solution seemed. Completely simple, but extremely delicate.

There were two magnetic sensors, one on the door frame and one on the door itself. When the door opened, the two pieces separated, lost contact, and that triggered the alarm.

So all I have to do is take off the door sensor and tape it to the other unit.

The problem was if she made a mistake, if her hand slipped, if she dropped a component, she would get them all arrested.

Melissa knew she was a whiz with electronics. At home, she had built her own computer from a kit. She could do this with her eyes closed and one hand tied behind her back.

But the stakes had never been this high, with so many other people involved. She was such a loner. Being part of a team was a whole new experience for her. Maybe she should ask the others, talk to Griffin.

She thought back to the green paper that had invited her to the first meeting in the Ballroom: *You have been chosen for your special skills* . . .

This was her skill. She was going to do this, to prove to herself as much as anybody else that she belonged on this team.

She ran to the kitchen and began rummaging around until she found the utility drawer. There, near the top, were the two items she'd been seeking — a small Phillips-head screwdriver and a roll of masking tape.

Back at the door, she propped up her flashlight on a hall table to illuminate her work area. Then she ran a circle of tape loosely around the two components. With the touch of a surgeon — good thing her gloves were tight and well fitted — she removed the two screws holding the smaller contact to the door. Now it was free, held in place only by the masking tape.

She was scared beyond belief, but her

174

hands were rock steady. With agonizing care, she moved the unattached component until it was touching its partner on the door frame. Another application of tape held the pair tightly together. There was just enough space for the door to open and close.

So far, so good. All that remained was to test it.

She unlocked the deadbolt, turned the knob, and opened the door about six inches. A blast of cool air assailed her, powered by the windy night. No alarm sounded. The thrill of her triumph was so overwhelming that she could scarcely keep from shouting.

If she *had* shouted, she might have awakened Ben, who was a mere six feet away, curled up asleep at his post in the bushes, like he was in a featherbed.

"Luthor, what's wrong?" Savannah asked the Doberman for the umpteenth time. "Why are you acting so strange?"

The dog whisperer had been trying to calm Luthor's nervous restlessness. It couldn't be done. Savannah prided herself on being able to read an animal's thoughts from its body language. But all she could get from Luthor was agitation. Even more upsetting, she couldn't shake the feeling that the creature was trying to tell her something important.

Whining and twitching, Luthor again grabbed her by the sleeve and began dragging her toward the staircase.

"Okay, I'm coming. Don't pull so hard." It was an effort to keep her feet as she was towed down the steps and across the checkered tile of the main hall. Scrambling to keep up, she realized that the dog had a very specific destination in mind — a makeshift office near the front of the house. The closer they got to the door, the jumpier Luthor became.

Intrigued, Savannah played her flashlight over the room. She almost missed it. Stretched out asleep on a small rug was the largest

German shepherd she'd ever seen. Even as she watched, the huge dog stirred and raised its massive head into the beam. Its eyes fixed on her, glowing.

Savannah Drysdale had never been afraid of an animal in her life. Yet the savagery she saw in this shepherd's eyes, coupled with the whimper of fear from the Doberman at her side, triggered a split-second decision. She slammed the door shut. The impact of a heavy body against the other side convinced her that she had done the right thing.

She took hold of Luthor's collar and raced back up the stairs. Full-throated barking resounded throughout the house.

She arrived, panting, in the master bed-room, where Griffin was partway through burning a large hole into the side of the safe. Acrid smoke hung in the air, and the metal glowed bright orange along the track made by the blowtorch.

Pitch sat on the bed, resting her injured

leg. "What's all that barking? What's the matter with Luthor?" Her bewildered gaze fell on the Doberman, standing docile at Savannah's side. "Oh —"

"There's another dog!" blurted Savannah. "I think it might be a trained attack dog!"

Griffin looked up in alarm. "Is it loose?"

"He's trapped in a room downstairs," Savannah quavered. "At least, I think it's a he. I can't imagine a female that size. I'm afraid he'll find a way to break through the door!"

"Can't you whisper him down?" Darren demanded. "That's supposed to be your job!"

"This isn't the time to try," Savannah insisted. "There are too many people around — intruders in a house he's trained to protect! Plus he could set off Luthor — the poor baby's terrified of this monster!"

With sinking hearts, the heist team realized that their dog whisperer was right. Savannah's words were punctuated by enraged barking and violent slams against a wooden door.

"Nobody panic," Griffin ordered. "Another few minutes and I'll be into the safe. We'll have our card, and Melissa has found us a way out — the plan is still on track."

Luthor's uneasy whimpers indicated that he didn't think so.

23

The backgammon tournament stood at 13–9 when the barking started.

"Listen to that racket," Eli Mulroney complained. "Leave it to Pal-o-Mine to have the two loudest dogs in creation."

Logan sprayed a mouthful of ginger ale all over himself. "*Two* dogs?"

The old man nodded in disgust. "I thought Luthor was bad enough. A couple of days ago, Pal-o-Mine brought in that Rent-a-Beast. Makes Luthor look like a hamster. I hear he's got some baseball card that's supposed to be valuable."

There was nothing Logan could do but continue the game and try not to think about what might be going on across the street. Besides, he reflected, the team had a look-out — Melissa — in the bushes. If things got too awful, Griffin would walkie-talkie her to go for help.

A shiny black SUV moved slowly up the street, its driver hanging out the window, peering at address numbers. It passed the Mulroney house, then made a U-turn and pulled up in front of the porch, big motor idling.

"Excuse me, sir. I'm looking for 531 Park Avenue Extension."

Mr. Mulroney pointed to the Palomino home. "That's it right there. Can't see a blamed thing with the streetlight out. The way they run this town should be a federal crime."

"Thanks." The SUV moved away from the curb, pulled into the Palomino driveway, and parked.

Mr. Mulroney handed Logan the dice. "Your turn — Logan? You look like you've just seen a ghost."

It was much worse than that. Logan was

watching the driver get out of the car and walk up the steps to Swindle's front door.

Griffin's eyes stung from the sweat pouring off his forehead and under his safety goggles. His stocking cap was drenched with perspiration. He had seen his father working with this blowtorch so many times. Never could he have imagined that it was so exhausting. Or maybe it was the excitement building inside him as he held the flame to the last quarter-inch of metal.

The thrill was indescribable. Barely a thread remained between him and the final realization of the greatest plan he would ever be a part of. It was so many things all at once — victory, justice, revenge. Not to mention a boatload of money.

And then the piece tumbled to the carpet, and he was staring in the open flank of the lockbox. Darren positioned his flashlight so Griffin could see inside. Careful not touch the red-hot edges of the hole, he reached in and removed the safe's contents.

There were some papers, a handful of collectible coins, and three hundred dollars in cash.

All five team members rifled through the box and everything that had been removed from it.

The Bambino was not there.

Darren put all their agony into words. "Bing, you idiot! Where's the card?"

"I thought it was in here!" Griffin shot back. He was almost too shocked and upset to argue with Darren. "I didn't burn into this thing for my health, you know!"

Pitch shook her head in grudging admiration. "That guy Swindle — he's one tough nut."

"He beat us," Savannah admitted sadly.

"This isn't over yet!" Griffin vowed. "The auction people expected to pick up that card today! It's in this house somewhere!"

"This is just great!" Darren seethed. "I nearly fell off the roof, there's a vicious dog chewing its way through a door, and now we've got no card. How could it be worse?"

The doorbell rang.

Lamar Fontaine pressed the button for the second time.

Ding-dong.

The house was dark, but he could have sworn he saw movement in a front room.

Besides, he was a bonded courier, entrusted with receiving and delivering an item worth as much as a million dollars. People did not stand him up, even when he was hours late.

He rang one more time and then tried the knob. It turned, and the door opened wide.

The feeling was too familiar — fighting his way through cotton wool, struggling with that terrible "where am I?" feeling. And then Swindle's front bush was all around Ben Slovak.

Oh, no! The heist!

There was hooting coming from across the street, and he struggled to remember what that might mean.

The signal!

Why would Logan be giving him the emergency signal?

He looked up and saw the answer. A tall man was letting himself in through the front door.

He pulled out his walkie-talkie and pressed the button. "Griffin — there's a guy coming into the house!"

"We know," came the whispered reply. "Is it Swindle?"

"No, definitely not Swindle. It must be somebody looking for Swindle."

Cautiously, Ben crept up the steps and peered inside through the side windows.

The newcomer was in the foyer. "Mr. Palomino?" called the man. "Courier service. Mr. Palomino . . ."

He crossed the hall and opened a door to peer inside.

What happened next was an image so horrifying that it would remain forever burned into Ben's memory.

24

A hulking animal exploded out of the room and pounced on the intruder. Terrified, the man swung his briefcase and cracked the German shepherd across the snout. Yelping with pain and rage, the dog fell back for an instant. By the time it gathered itself for another charge, Lamar Fontaine was high-tailing it across the tiles toward the basement steps. He slammed the door behind him a split second before the shepherd plowed into it, howling with fury as it re-injured its sore nose.

It was preparing for another run when it

heard a bark from above. That brought the guard dog galloping upstairs.

Ben sounded the warning, for all the good it was going to do. "Griffin! All of you! *Hide!*"

But there was no time for hiding, or even thinking. The rest of the team was trapped in the master bedroom. The shepherd appeared in the doorway, menacing them all and cutting off any avenue of escape.

The dog whisperer stepped forward. "Hi, big guy," she said in her most soothing tone. "You don't want to hurt anybody. We're all friends here. Let's not get ex —"

With a malevolent roar, the monster leaped at her. Seeing Savannah in danger, Luthor flung himself into the path of the attacking shepherd. The two dogs met in midair and fell, snarling and wrestling, to the floor.

The heist team wasted no time getting out of the room and down the stairs, Griffin and Darren half carrying Pitch.

Ben met them on the midway landing. "There's a dog after you, and it isn't Luthor!"

"Quick! The kitchen!" ordered Savannah.

Darren was wild-eyed. "Why? Are you going to whip up a soufflé?"

"I'm going to find some meat to distract that brute from killing poor Luthor!"

Nobody gave her an argument. In a fight with the much larger shepherd, the Doberman was David facing Goliath. There was no question that Luthor had risked his life to protect Savannah.

The team hit the main floor and ran into the kitchen. Savannah ripped open the freezer and began rummaging for meat.

"Any steaks?" Ben asked helpfully. "Dogs love steak."

"I can't find anything! This is in the way!" She lifted out an enormous frozen turkey and dumped it on the tiles.

And there, in the middle of all that chaos, a strange calm descended over Griffin. It tuned out his heist-mates, and even the fact that there were two warring dogs one flight up. He heard his own voice from days before: *Oh,*

189

sure! Like a nasty, obnoxious crook knows enough people willing to sit down and eat a twenty-pound turkey with him! And that expert on the web clip, holding the card, asking: *Why is it so cold?*

Suddenly, he was on his knees over the frozen bird, reaching his hand into the breast cavity.

Darren was disgusted. "I always knew you were crazy, Bing, but I never thought you were the type to go digging in a turkey's butt!"

In answer, Griffin pulled out a Ziploc baggie. There was a picture peering through the clear plastic.

Babe Ruth in a Boston Red Sox uniform.

Savannah pulled the shrink-wrap off two T-bone steaks. She ran to the bottom of the staircase and flung them up to the top landing. In an instant, the two dogs had forgotten about each other and were chewing on the cold, hard meat.

Griffin removed the card from the Ziploc

and held it lovingly. "This is the greatest moment of my life."

"Yeah, mine too!" Darren snatched the prize out of his hand and ran for the front door. "Sayonara, suckers!"

It was so shocking, so unexpected, that the team just stood there, openmouthed, and watched him go.

Then, total wild action — a stampede in hot pursuit. Even Pitch was running full-tilt, hopping and limping through her pain.

Griffin led the charge. Of all the things he'd planned for, all the *in case of*s and *what if*s, how could he have overlooked the most obvious possibility — a double cross from one of his own people? Especially Darren, who had always been an enemy and an untrustworthy jerk.

But what a price to pay for one mistake!

Darren pounded down the front steps. Griffin followed, losing his breath momentarily to a gust of wind. Hot on his friend's heels, Ben vaulted up onto the porch rail and hurled himself like a flying squirrel at Darren's fleeing form.

He missed the takedown, but his flailing arm caught Darren on the ankle. The big boy lost his balance and hit the ground like a ton of bricks. The Babe Ruth card popped out of his hand.

Suddenly, the Bambino was airborne, riding a mammoth blast of wind. The team watched in agony as the million-dollar collectible fluttered higher and higher, swirling on the turbulent air currents. The wind played with it for a few more seconds before depositing it in the lacy upper branches of a very tall maple tree.

With a cry of frustration, Darren got up, rushed to the trunk, and began climbing like a madman.

Griffin turned to Pitch.

"No way," she said, reading his mind. "Not with this ankle. And I don't want any of you idiots trying it. You'll wind up dead, and

192

probably so will he." She cupped her hands to her mouth. "Darren, you'll never make it!"

"What about the ladder?" Ben suggested.

"Not high enough," Pitch told him. "That tree towers over the house."

Griffin was nearly insane. "It's a million-dollar card! There must be some way to get to it!"

"Dream on," Savannah said unhappily. "Not unless you've got some miracle tool that can reach forty feet up, pick out the tiniest thing, and bring it back down safely."

The look of shocked realization on Griffin Bing's face was like nothing anyone had ever seen before.

W ith the streetlight out, no one could see what was happening at the Palomino house. But there was no mistaking the sound of scuffling feet and raised voices. Some kind of commotion was going on across the street.

Eli Mulroney jumped to his feet. "What the blazes —"

Logan was bewildered. He and the team had been over the plan so many times, and no part of it included running around outside and yelling. The plan must have jumped off the rails somehow, but he couldn't admit that here. So he said with a straight face, "I don't hear anything."

But obviously he didn't "sell" the line, because the old man slapped a fist into his palm. "That does it! This neighborhood is going down the drain. It's gotten to the point where a man can't enjoy a few quiet moments on his front porch! I'm calling the police!"

Whatever was going on, Logan knew he had to do something. In theater lingo, it was called an ad-lib — when an actor broke from the script and followed his gut for the good of the show. It was time for a beauty right now.

Logan braced both feet flat on the floorboards and launched himself rearward with all his might. The rocker swung back and flipped over, tossing him off the porch and into a bank of juniper bushes.

"God bless America! Logan, are you okay?"

The young actor was better than okay. While the old man was dabbing iodine on Logan's many cuts and scratches, no one was calling the police.

What a performance!

*　　*　　*

He had just covered the better part of a mile in a full sprint, but Griffin felt none of the ache in his legs or the fire in his lungs.

He approached his own home almost as stealthily as he had Swindle's. As far as Mom and Dad knew, Griffin was at Ben's — a marathon work session on a science fair project.

The garage could be opened from the outside by keypad code. The mechanism whirred to life and the door began to roll up and away. It seemed louder than a twenty-car pileup, but no one came bursting out to investigate the noise. Maybe Mom and Dad were too absorbed in one of their spirited checkbook-balancing sessions to notice.

He shrugged out of the acetylene tank and entered the garage, setting the blowtorch kit down on the concrete. The only light was the dim glow coming in from the streetlamp. Farther in, it was pitch-dark. He bumped the edge of his father's workbench and held his breath as tools jarred and resettled. A few screws or bolts pinged against the cement floor.

Griffin felt around the blackness until his hand closed on the aluminum pole. It was time to give the SmartPick its first true test.

Opting for speed over stealth, he jumped on his bike, the device balanced on his lap as he pedaled for Swindle's house. He crossed town in record time, very nearly losing his father's invention as he wheeled onto Park Avenue Extension.

It was hard to see anything in the area of the broken streetlight, but the clamor of excited voices was unmistakable. He jumped off his bike and ran onto the scene, squinting as his eyes adjusted to the dark. He thought he spied Darren halfway up the heavy trunk. But no — the figure was too small. It was Pitch, climbing gingerly and grimacing in pain with every movement of her injured ankle.

He ran up to Ben, who stood with the

197

other team members, gazing at the big maple. "Where's Darren?"

Ben pointed. "Maybe he really *is* part gorilla."

Griffin gawked. No wonder he hadn't spotted Darren at first. The big boy was thirty feet up, barely a body-length below the Babe Ruth card. He clung to a narrow branch, swaying in the wind as he shinnied ever closer to the million-dollar prize.

Savannah regarded the SmartPick dubiously. "You sure picked a strange time for a fishing trip."

"It's my dad's invention! It can get us the card! Hey, why did you guys let Pitch go up there with her bad leg?"

The drama unfolding in the tree had unmasked Melissa. Her curtain of hair was permanently parted, her wide eyes riveted on the two climbers. "I don't think she's after the card. I think she's trying to rescue Darren."

"Looks like Darren's doing just fine on his

198

own," Ben observed nervously. "Another few feet, and he's got it."

With that, Darren pulled himself forward on the undulating branch and reached for the Bambino. His probing fingers passed just a few inches beneath it.

Griffin powered on the SmartPick and pressed the button. With a low whir, the aluminum pole telescoped outward, soaring high above them into the night.

It works! he thought in amazement. Not that he'd doubted his father. Yet never could he have imagined that it would be so impressive. The air was filled with blowing leaves. Trees rolled and weaved with the wind. But the SmartPick never wavered, rising laser-straight into the maple's branches.

"What the —?" Pitch did a double take as the gleaming metal whizzed past her shoulder.

"Wow," breathed Ben. "Your old man really *is* a genius!"

Griffin shuffled his feet and tried to aim the FruitSafe pincers at the tiny card. Every

199

motion on the ground translated into a major swing on the other end of the long pole. The picking mechanism pitched wildly as it neared the top of the tree.

Darren shuffled a little farther on his branch. He extended his arm and felt his fingertips brush the edge of the card. This was it!

As he braced for the final stretch that would make him a millionaire, a metallic ring rose up right in front of him. The device opened into rubber-tipped pincers that closed delicately on the Babe Ruth card and, with a twist, plucked it from the branch.

His eyes bulged in dismay. *The — the — DumbPick?!*

He snatched at the Bambino, but the pincers had already begun to retract, bearing the collectible away. There was a sickly cracking sound.

Uh-oh . . .

Far below, the team watched in tense anticipation as the prize made its descent.

"Careful," Ben said anxiously. "Don't rip it."

Griffin hung on to the SmartPick like a fisherman landing a shark in the middle of a full gale. "Don't worry. The patented FruitSafe mechanism is guaranteed not to damage fruit."

"That's not fruit," Savannah pointed out. "That's my vet school tuition, Melissa's computer, Logan's acting lessons, Pitch's climbing trip. College paid for, new cars when we're old enough —"

Melissa wore a grin so wide it nearly split her face. "I can't believe we actually did it!"

And then a voice from above called, "*He-e-elp!*"

26

Darren was falling, still clutching the useless limb as it tore away from the tree. The team watched helplessly as he plummeted toward them. Ten feet up, the ripping wood held suddenly firm. Darren cried out as the branch lurched violently and swung around in the direction of the house.

Crash!

The bough slammed into a downstairs window, shattering the glass and tossing the boy like a rag doll back into the Palomino home.

An earsplitting wail blasted through the neighborhood as the UltraTech alarm system burst to life. Griffin abandoned the SmartPick and joined Ben, Savannah, and Melissa in a mad dash for the house. Pitch dropped from the tree and limped after them.

Griffin could taste bitter dread boiling up in his throat. He peered in to see Darren sprawled in the wreckage of the window, unmoving.

Oh my God, is he dead?

And then the big boy rolled over, shook his fist, and started shouting with rage. The rush of relief nearly knocked Griffin over. He couldn't imagine ever being so happy to be yelled at by this jerk.

With Melissa's help, he hauled Darren over the sill. Except for torn clothing and cuts and bruises, their betrayer was unhurt.

"You okay?" Pitch bawled in his ear. And when Darren nodded sheepishly, she hauled off and punched him in the stomach.

Logan pounded onto the wild scene, hollering like a madman. It was impossible to hear him over the clamor of the siren, but his meaning could not be mistaken: This outdoor chaos wasn't part of the plan. What had gone wrong?

Griffin grabbed him by the shoulders. "You were supposed to stay with Mr. Mulroney!"

"You think he'd sit through this kind of noise?" the actor shouted back. "He went inside to call the cops, so I took off! Did we get the card?"

The card! The SmartPick was lying on the ground somewhere, with a million-dollar payload in its pincers.

Griffin retraced his steps, desperately scanning the grass. He could see nothing in the darkness.

This can't be happening . . . not when we're so close —

A glint of metal caught his attention. Heart pounding, he snatched up his father's invention. The Bambino was still nestled in the mechanism.

The alarm's gut-churning howl died abruptly. After such overpowering noise, the sudden silence was as explosive as a bomb blast. The unexpected quiet revealed two sounds: police sirens in the distance and the barking of a guard dog — no, *two* guard dogs —

"*Code Z!*" Griffin bellowed.

There was a code Z in all Griffin's plans — the escape clause. The moment when the operation was either completed, or busted, or both, and all that remained was to get the heck out of there.

The team scattered.

"Hey!" cried Darren. "Somebody's got to help me with my ladder!"

"In your dreams!" snorted Pitch, who was limping at top speed, indicating that her ankle felt a little better.

Darren raced to the side of the house and tried to pull the twenty-four-foot length away from the wall. The top overbalanced, and he had to dive to safety as the entire thing fell with a resounding *kong* to the grass. Chest heaving, he began the process of collapsing the six-foot sections and snapping them into place.

The second piece wouldn't budge. Frantically, he tried to stomp it down. "Come *on*!"

He made a split-second decision and ran after the others. "Wait up!" If those two dogs found the broken window, he didn't like his chances of outrunning them with a ladder on his back. And that same ladder was going to look pretty suspicious if the cops caught him with it on their way to investigate a rooftop break-in. Nothing was free in this world, and the cost of tonight was one ladder. He'd explain it to his parents somehow — even if he had to tell them Griffin Bing stole it.

Griffin stuffed the card in his pocket, and he and Ben made a beeline for the bike. "Hold this!" Griffin commanded, handing over the SmartPick. "And try to stay awake this time!" And they were off, riding double along Park Avenue Extension, swerving down a side street to avoid an approaching squad car.

Ben was frantic. "What if Swindle figures out it was us? The police will search us and find the card!"

Griffin cruised up and stopped beside a mailbox. "I've got it covered." He reached inside his shirt and produced an envelope with the address and stamp already on it. He popped the Bambino inside, sealed the flap, and dropped the letter through the slot.

Ben was bug-eyed. "You *mailed* it? To who?"

"It's better for you not to know."

They got back on the bike and rode to Ben's house. Ben jumped off and handed over the SmartPick. "I've always had a lot of respect for you, man," he said solemnly. "But I never dreamed we had a prayer of pulling off what we did tonight!"

"If you've got the right plan," Griffin told him, "that's all you need."

Just the thought of a successful operation brought a smile to his lips. As he pedaled toward home he allowed himself a few moments of self-congratulation. True, there had been hiccups — Pitch's injury, Ben's catnap, the empty safe, the extra dog, the guy at the door, and especially Darren's betrayal. But the team had improvised, sidestepped, overcome. After all, the team was part of the plan. And this had been the plan to end all plans.

As he rounded the corner to his own block, his heart very nearly jumped out of his rib cage. Dancing colored lights whirled across the brick front of the Bing house. A squad car was parked in the driveway, flashers ablaze.

27

He was astounded. How could the cops be here already? The team had gotten away before any officers reached the Palomino home to investigate the alarm. And Swindle should still be at the hockey game . . .

For a moment, Griffin actually thought about turning his bike around and making a break for it. How crazy was that? A fugitive, living on the lam, never to see his family or friends again? No, there was nothing to do but face the music and hope for the best. At least he didn't have the card on him. The police couldn't prove anything without that.

Steeling himself, he ditched his gloves and stocking cap in a bush, and pedaled for home.

"Hey! *Hey!*" Two uniformed officers were running across the lawn. A third figure was right behind them. Dad.

Before Griffin could dismount, the larger of the cops grabbed him under the arms and hauled him bodily off the bike. The man's partner snatched the SmartPick and held it up to Mr. Bing.

"Sir, is this the prototype that was stolen from your garage?"

Stolen? The truth came crashing down on Griffin. This had nothing to do with the robbery! Dad must have gone to investigate the noises coming from the garage. When he found his invention missing, he called the cops.

Mr. Bing looked shocked and embarrassed. "I'm sorry, officers. It seems I've been wasting your time. This is my son." To Griffin, he said, "What were you doing with my prototype?"

Griffin was so relieved to be off the hook for the baseball card that he had a hard time working up a shamefaced expression. "Ben wanted to see how it worked. We were just picking pinecones out of trees."

The senior officer spoke up. "You weren't anywhere near Park Ex, were you? We've had reports of some vandalism over there. Broken window, alarm signal."

Mr. Bing stepped in. "No, his friend's house is nowhere near there. I'm afraid this is all my mistake. I apologize for dragging you over here."

Griffin withered under his father's disapproving gaze as the officers got back in their car and drove away.

Mr. Bing returned the invention to its place in his workshop. "You nearly gave me a heart attack," he said finally. "When I stepped into the garage and the prototype wasn't there, I just about lost it. I've poured my blood and sweat into that baby — not to mention most of our savings."

Griffin studied his sneakers. "Sorry, Dad." But what he wanted to say was: *We're going*

to have more than enough money to develop
your invention — and we won't have to sell
the house to do it.

"What were you thinking? If you and Ben wanted a demonstration, all you had to do was ask." A ghost of a smile tugged at his lip. "So, how did it go? Did the prototype perform up to expectations?"

It was like a sequence from a movie — the telescoping pole defying gravity to snatch the card away from Darren in the nick of time. "Oh, Dad," he said earnestly. "In a million years, I never would have believed what a SmartPick can do!"

The text message came halfway through the second period of the Rangers–Maple Leafs game:

ULTRATECH SECURITY
E-ALERT SYSTEM
TIME OF ALERT: 8:47 P.M.

**ATTENTION: PALOMINO, S. WENDELL
AN ALARM SIGNAL HAS BEEN
RECEIVED FROM THE FOLLOWING
ADDRESS: 531 PARK AVENUE
EXTENSION, CEDARVILLE, NY
ULTRATECH CENTRAL STATION
MONITORING HAS REPORTED THE
INCIDENT TO POLICE**

Never before had the highways of New York City seen a Honda Element driving at such reckless speeds. Weaving in and out of traffic, S. Wendell Palomino streaked eastward toward the Cedarville exit. He was still doing at least sixty as he screeched to a halt inches from the police cruiser in his driveway.

The dealer was already breathing hard as he rushed up the front steps and fixed his sunny-side-up eyes on the officer positioned at the door.

"You're the homeowner?" she inquired.

Palomino nodded, but stood there wheezing, incapable of speech.

"There's been a break-in," the officer informed him. "The entry point was from the roof through the bathroom skylight. It looks like the thieves got what they were after. Your safe has been burned open, probably by blowtorch."

"Never mind the safe!" Palomino babbled frantically. "What about my turkey?"

"Your *turkey*?"

The agitated dealer blew by her and ran into the kitchen, where a horrifying sight greeted him. What had once been a twenty-pound turkey was now perhaps a three-pound skeleton. Luthor and the hired German shepherd lay side by side on the tile floor, too stuffed with ice-cold meat to do more than raise their heads and growl.

"We found one suspect hiding in the basement, a Mr. Lamar Fontaine. But he seems to be unconnected to the crime. His ID says he works for an auction company. We think he walked in on the robbery, and the dogs chased him down there. He's pretty shaken up."

"But what about the *real* thieves?" Palomino wailed. "Why didn't the dogs go after *them*?"

"Impossible to tell," the officer replied. "The turkey was probably used as a distraction."

Palomino knew the truth was much more awful than that. He could see right through the turkey ribs that the chest cavity was empty. Discarded on the counter was the Ziploc bag that had kept the card clean and dry inside the frozen bird.

The Bambino was gone.

28

THIEVES NAB $1M CARD ON EVE OF AUCTION

In what is being called the most spectacular robbery in the history of sports collectibles, a 1920 baseball card valued as high as $1,000,000 was stolen from its owner's home last night. The rare card, which portrayed slugger Babe Ruth as a member of the Boston Red Sox during his first season as a Yankee, was taken by thieves who dropped from a skylight wearing climbing harnesses.

The daring heist was carried out under the noses of two trained guard dogs and a bonded courier hired by Worthington's Auction House, where the card was to be sold scarcely twelve hours later. Police are investigating leads, including the harnesses and an extension ladder found at the scene. . . .

216

Quiet, sleepy Cedarville was suddenly on the map. TV news mobile units wandered the town, searching for Park Avenue Extension and Palomino's Emporium. A fleet of vans equipped with satellite dishes formed in front of West Suffolk Medical Center, where S. Wendell Palomino had gone, suffering from nervous collapse.

"I didn't expect so much publicity," Ben mumbled worriedly at school on Friday. "Every time you turn on the TV, there's Swindle tearing his hair and weeping."

"Get real — it's a million bucks," retorted Darren. "What I want to know is how long do we have to lie low before we can sell the card and get our money."

"*Your* money?" Pitch was indignant. "You tried to rip the rest of us off. I don't see why you should get a cent."

"Because I can turn you in to the cops," Darren said smugly. "Like it or not, we're in this together."

Griffin didn't relish the idea of Darren profiting from his betrayal. But he had to admit his enemy had a point. They *were* in this together. All day, the heist team clung to one another like shipwreck victims adrift in a small lifeboat.

When Ben headed down to the nurse for his "allergy medicine," he made sure to stop by the media center to check the TV monitor. "We made CNN," he reported after his catnap. "The sound was off, but in the scrolling headlines, they called it a 'professional job.'"

"Well, that could be good news," Griffin mused cautiously. "Professional means they probably don't suspect kids."

"Guys," Savannah called in a strangled voice. "Look."

The team joined her at the window. Two police cruisers were pulling up the circular drive of the school.

Melissa's haunted eyes took refuge behind her curtain of hair.

"Maybe there's a safety assembly today," Logan suggested hopefully.

Oh, how Griffin wished for it to be so.

A few minutes later, the PA system burst to life. *"Would Darren Vader report to the office, please? Darren Vader to the office."*

With a sinking heart, Griffin told himself that there were a million reasons for a jerk like Darren to be in trouble. But he knew it was the ladder.

How could we just leave it there at the crime scene?

At the time it had seemed like Darren's problem and Darren's only. Now he realized that one member could be the police's stepping-stone to the entire team.

Griffin waited in agony for Darren to return to the classroom. He never came back. Savannah communicated the news through panic-stricken eyes. From her seat by the window, she had a perfect view of Darren being driven home by his parents.

"Would Antonia Benson report to the office, please? Antonia Benson."

"What's with our class today?" joked Mr. Martinez. "Did you guys rob a bank or something?" He frowned at the raw fear on Pitch's ashen face as she limped to the door. "I was only kidding."

Griffin had a chilling vision — a pile of nylon ropes tethered to a broken vent pipe, sitting in Swindle's bathroom. Everybody in Cedarville knew the Bensons were the only climbing family in town. Of course the cops had put two and two together.

Was the perfect operation unraveling before their very eyes?

Like Darren, Pitch did not return to class. The other members of the team spent the remainder of the day in stiff-necked misery, wondering whose name would be called next. But as of the three-thirty dismissal, the PA system had remained mercifully silent.

After school, all Griffin could offer was an appeal for calm. "I admit that it doesn't look good, but the last thing we can afford is panic. Remember, we don't know anything for sure yet."

It was a measure of just how frightened everyone was that there was no babble of disagreement in the ranks of the guilty. At this point, there was nothing left to do but hope.

On the walk home, though, Ben could not keep silent. "How bad is it, Griffin? I mean, if the cops find out everything, how much trouble are we in?"

"Impossible to tell," said Griffin soberly. "On the one hand, we're kids. On the other, breaking into a house is a real crime. And the thing we took is worth a ton of money. I've got a bad feeling about this media attention."

They went their separate ways, and Griffin continued home, dragging his feet, not at all anxious to get there. He was genuinely amazed not to see half the police force camped out on his doorstep waiting for him.

"How was school today?" his mother greeted.

He looked over her shoulder. No army of cops ransacking the place in search of the missing collectible. "Oh, you know, same old, same old." He prayed that the situation would stay that way. No news was good news.

He set out his homework, but could not bring himself to touch it. It would have been too much like that Roman emperor fiddling while his city burned. Four o'clock. All clear. Four-thirty. Still nothing. Was it possible that they were going to get away with it?

He was so tightly strung that when the phone rang, he almost hit the ceiling.

It was Pitch. "I'm not supposed to be talking to you. Listen — I ratted you out." *Oh, no! Oh, no! Oh, no!* "I'm really, really sorry. My parents made me. And I'm pretty sure Darren did the same."

Oh, no, no, no-o-o-o!!

Beneath his full-on panic, he was aware of a strange sense of relief — the terrified relief a soldier might feel when the waiting is over and the battle has finally begun. At least he wouldn't have to waste his energy wishing for miracles.

"Don't sweat it, Pitch," he croaked bravely. "Thanks for the heads-up."

Through his bedroom window he could already see the line of police cars turning onto his street. There was very little chance that they were going to someone else's house.

The jig was up.

29

BEING INTERROGATED BY POLICE —
HELPFUL HINTS

Stick like GLUE to the THREE ANSWERS:

(i) I DIDN'T STEAL IT. You can't steal
what's already yours.

(ii) I DON'T HAVE IT. A search of the
house will prove this is the truth.

(iii) I DON'T KNOW WHERE IT IS. Also
true, since it's impossible to tell if the card
is still in the mailbox, at the post office, or
on its way to the destination address.

G riffin never put the latest plan on paper, but it was very much in his mind when the police came to question him in the case of the stolen Babe Ruth card.

It wasn't much like cop shows on TV. There were no handcuffs, no hot lights in the face, no one-way mirrors. In fact, they didn't even go to the precinct house. The interrogation took place in the Bings' living room, with Griffin flanked by his parents on the couch.

Detective Sergeant Vizzini was polite, but it was obvious that he was losing patience. "Maybe you think that a little baseball card is something to collect and trade and flick at a brick wall. Well, not this one. This one is worth more than a house. This very minute, in New York City, a major auction is a big flop because this card was supposed to be the main event."

"I didn't steal anything," Griffin said stubbornly.

"That's not what Darren Vader said.

That's not what the Benson girl said. Two of my officers were here last night when you arrived home with your father's thingama-jig. The timing would have been just about right. I've been a cop too long to believe in coincidences."

Dad spoke up. "Griffin, if you know something about this, you have to tell the sergeant right now."

"There's nothing to tell," Griffin insisted, trying to keep his voice steady. "There are ten policemen tearing the place apart. If I was hiding a baseball card in the house, wouldn't they have found it by now?"

"So enlighten me," Vizzini demanded. "It wasn't in your desk or your locker at school, and it doesn't seem to be here. What did you do with it?"

"I don't know where it is."

Vizzini frowned. "Are you denying that you were at 531 Park Avenue Extension last night?"

226

"I haven't done anything wrong," Griffin said firmly. "Not by stealing, not by lying about it."

The officer digested this. When he spoke again, it was to Griffin's parents. "I'm going to give you two some time to talk things over with your son. You'll notice that I haven't been using words like arrest, trial, or juvenile detention. Yet."

Mr. Bing looked up in alarm. "Does Griffin need a lawyer?"

"Well, that would be up to you folks. Just take a minute to think about what Mr. Palomino has lost. If you were him, would you be inclined to say 'Drat the luck' and let the matter drop? I don't think so." He stood up. "Until this issue is resolved, Griffin is not to leave the Cedarville town limits. He can go to school, but that's about as far from home as we're willing to allow. Otherwise we *will* start using words like *arrest*."

With that promise hanging in the air like a

cloud of toxic fumes, Vizzini gathered his team of searchers and left the house.

"All right, Griffin," Dad said as the squad cars drove away. "I want the whole story."

Griffin knew he owed his parents the truth — and not just because there was no way to get out of telling it. The police had invaded their home, rifled through their belongings, threatened their son with imprisonment. Mom and Dad had become a part of this.

He came clean. "Remember that sleepover at Stan Winter's? Well, it never really happened. Ben and I spent the last night in the old Rockford house before they tore it down. . . ."

His parents listened, their eyes widening in awe and amazement as their son related the details of the discovery of the Babe Ruth card, and how Swindle had earned his nickname by tricking Griffin into selling it cheaply. He confessed everything — the unsuccessful break-in at the store, the assembly of the team, and the heist preparations, right up to the assault on 531 Park Avenue Extension.

"But where's the card now?" Dad demanded. "Where did you hide it that half the police department can't find it?"

"It's safe," Griffin assured him. "I wasn't lying when I told Officer Vizzini that I don't know exactly where it is. But I'll be able to get it when the time comes."

"The time is this minute!" Mom stormed. "I can't believe we're even having this conversation! When you were growing up, did we somehow give you the message that stealing is okay?"

"Of course not!" Griffin exclaimed. "That's why I did it — so Swindle wouldn't get away with stealing it from me. Think about what that card is worth!"

"I don't care what it's worth," she shot back. "Your future is worth more! Stop playing games and give the police what they want!"

Mr. Bing tried to be reasonable. "How about this? We give the police the card to get you off the hook. Then we hire a lawyer and fight this Palomino character in court."

229

"Get real, Dad. You know we can't afford lawyers. That's what this whole thing was about in the first place — to get our hands on some money so we won't have to sell the house." There was a shocked silence. "Oh, come on, guys. There's a FOR SALE sign on our lawn. Give me a little credit for having the brains to figure out what it's doing there."

When he spoke again, Mr. Bing's face was almost gray. "I know we've had our money problems. But your mother and I never dreamed that it would touch you this way."

"Don't blame yourselves. We shouldn't even *have* money problems. That card is *ours*!"

Mrs. Bing was close to tears. "Oh, Griffin, how could you get yourself into such a mess?"

Throughout the planning and execution of the heist, Griffin had never suffered a single moment of regret. Now, as he saw his parents' distress, adding to their burdens this way cut straight to his heart.

Later, he sat in his room in semidarkness, trying to tune out the sound of his parents'

argument downstairs. For once, the subject wasn't money. It was what to do with their son the burglar.

It now dawned on him for the very first time: He had plotted the operation with the skill of a chess master. But he had given very little thought to what would happen once the Bambino was in his possession. Had he expected Swindle to give up without a fight? And the police to shrug the whole thing off after their first search turned up nothing? That was bad enough, but he had also given zero consideration to his parents. Like maybe they simply wouldn't notice that anything unusual was going on.

Was he crazy, or just stupid? He certainly didn't have the right to call himself The Man With The Plan anymore.

Mom's voice carried up the stairs. "We have to force him to give up that card! It's our job as his parents to see that he doesn't destroy his life! He's only eleven years old!"

Her husband's words were quieter and full

of despair. "We can order him, we can yell at him, ground him, and lock him in his room. But if he doesn't want to tell us, there's absolutely nothing we can do about it."

It shocked Griffin a little, but he instantly recognized that his father was right. In spite of all the adults involved, only Griffin was capable of laying hands on the Bambino. And there was no way his parents, or Swindle, or the auction house, or the police, or even the president could change that.

This should have made him feel powerful. Instead, he felt trapped, and very much alone.

30

Ben called on Saturday morning, but Griffin was afraid to say much. What if the police had bugged their phone?

"So, uh, Ben — did anything unusual happen yesterday? Any *visitors* at your house?"

"Oh, yeah," Ben replied nervously. "I think we all had . . . visitors. They talked about you a lot. The visitors, I mean. Are you all right?"

"Kind of," Griffin told him. "For now. You?"

"I'm still part deaf in one ear from my mother yelling." There was an awkward pause. "How about the apple?"

Griffin subjected him to a long silence. "I don't know anything about any apple." He was dying to say: *It's okay. It's still hidden. It's safe.* But there was no way he could risk mentioning the card now. At this moment, it might be the single hottest item in the greater New York area.

"Oh . . . yeah. Gotcha," Ben stammered. "Have you seen the paper? There's a lot about what happened, but they don't mention any names. That's good news, right?"

Griffin sighed. "I don't know what's good news or bad news anymore."

The only good news was not being arrested. He expected it to happen at any second. He could hear distant police sirens in every ordinary household sound — the power hum of the computer, the whir of the microwave, the refrigerator motor. He spent the weekend in a state of constant terror, sleeping no more than five or ten minutes at a stretch.

He was truly astonished still to be a free man when school resumed on Monday morning. It took an enormous mustering of courage to appear in the halls. But, to his surprise and relief, all eyes did not instantly dart to him. True, the heist was the big story in Cedarville. Yet it did not seem to be known who the prime suspects were. Maybe that made sense. Wasn't it typical of the adult world not to consider that kids could pull off such an elaborate operation?

The other team members — Pitch, Savannah, Melissa, Logan, and Darren — kept their distance. Everyone understood that the heat was on.

"They're probably under orders from their folks to stay away from you," Ben offered. "I sure am. It was one of the first things my mother yelled. Sort of stupid, right? I mean, the police already know who we are."

"Don't worry," Griffin promised. "I'll take all the blame. My plan, my problem." He looked around uneasily. "To be honest, I can't believe the cops haven't come for me yet."

"Did you see the story in the Sunday paper?" Ben asked. "It just about accused Swindle of ripping somebody off to get the card in the first

235

place. The whole country's going to learn what a crook he is."

Griffin winced. "That means one of us has been talking too much. Probably Darren. It's one thing to answer a few questions, and another to give a play-by-play of the whole operation. That same article had a long description of the SmartPick plucking the card out of Swindle's tree. Anybody can check with the patent office and find out that's my dad's invention. And that could lead them to me. I'm toast!"

But that was the astounding thing: He *wasn't* toast. Although Griffin's fevered imagination conjured up a police officer behind every telephone pole, Detective Sergeant Vizzini did not come back for him. Not that day, not Tuesday, not even Wednesday. People were still buzzing about the missing baseball card, but the world kept on turning.

Even S. Wendell Palomino had been released from the hospital and could now be found behind the counter of his shop. There weren't many customers. Word had spread that the dealer could not be trusted.

Griffin held that fact to his heart. It was a glowing coal on an icy night, a tiny measure of justice.

Did that mean the intense heat was beginning to cool off? Was it crazy to believe such a thing? Even Mom and Dad let Ben come over for a couple of hours so they could work on their science project together. At least, Mom said okay. Dad was making himself pretty scarce lately. Griffin couldn't escape the feeling that his father was avoiding him out of anger and distress over this whole affair. It made him unutterably sad.

"Have you been noticing the others talking to me in school?" Ben whispered during their research. "They're asking what's going on with the — you know, the apple."

"Tell them to hang in there," Griffin advised. "This isn't over yet."

"You mean you've got it?"

"I know where to get it," Griffin replied cryptically.

Ben couldn't hold back. "Where'd you mail it to, Griffin? Who's keeping it for us?"

"It's not a good idea for you to know."

It was a measure of their friendship that there was no suspicion in Ben's eyes. He trusted Griffin absolutely and had faith in The Man With The Plan.

"When do you think it's safe to go for it? It's been almost a week now. How long do we have to wait?"

That was the million-dollar question. The coast seemed to be clear. But how could it be? The passage of six days didn't mean that the heist had never happened. And the revelation that Swindle deserved what he got didn't undo the fact that the card had been taken from his house.

And yet — where were the police? Not at the Bing home. Not at the school. Griffin still couldn't shake the feeling that he was being watched, but it was exactly that — a feeling.

The facts suggested that the cops must have moved on to other things. All crime didn't grind to a halt just because a baseball card got stolen. They had new cases, laws to enforce, police business to attend to.

I hope.

Griffin knew that the longer he waited, the safer he would be. He also knew that the more time the card was out there, the greater the chance that something might happen to it.

He analyzed the situation every which way, and the answer always came back the same.

The moment was now.

31

Three a.m.

A black-clad figure opened the Bings' back door and stepped onto the patio. Staying in the shadows, he made his way down the street through yards, hopping fences and squeezing through hedges. At the end of his block, he allowed himself the luxury of the sidewalk, but kept well away from the streetlights.

The windows were dark, the roads deserted. He could see it now in the gloom, a quarter mile up the avenue. Every day on the way to school, he had passed this spot and made a point of not looking at it. Not yet. Not under the prying eyes of the police. But tonight no one was watching. There was only Griffin Bing, and — he hoped — George Herman "Babe" Ruth.

The debris was gone, but the stone foundation of the old Rockford house glowed stark whitish-gray in the moonlight. At the curb stood the only other part of the mansion that had escaped the wrecking ball — the mailbox, rusting on its post.

As he reached for the little door, Griffin observed his hand shaking.

What if it isn't there?

What if some sensible postal carrier had refused to deliver to a house that was obviously demolished?

No. The flag's up. It's been up for three days. There's mail in here — my mail . . .

He drew out the contents of the box and stared. *A free month of Netflix?* Wait — there was another envelope. A smaller one.

A million-dollar letter.

He tore it open and dropped the Babe Ruth card into his hand.

241

The floodlights were so sudden, so blinding that he was frozen in place like a butterfly on a pin. Detective Sergeant Vizzini stepped out of the glare and snatched the collectible from his hand. In that moment, Griffin understood that the eyes on the back of his neck had been real after all.

Vizzini spoke the words Griffin had been dreading for six days: "You're under arrest."

They didn't lock him in a cell. They didn't lock him up at all. He sat on a hard wooden chair in the middle of the squad room while Vizzini pounded out a report on a manual typewriter that must have been one hundred years old.

He knew he was in big trouble, though, because every single officer on the night shift came by to have a look at the kid who took down a house with an UltraTech alarm system and two guard dogs and made off with a million-dollar prize.

Caught. Just the word made him shudder. In a plan like this, so many factors were at play. But *caught* was always rock bottom. The worst thing that could have happened had just happened. There was no countermove for this, no recovery. This was a major disaster.

How many times had he told himself that it wasn't really stealing, that the card rightfully belonged to him? Here in the police station, he realized that argument wasn't going to work for five seconds. Griffin had always tried to stand up against adults pushing kids around. But now, under arrest, he had put himself more at the adults' mercy than ever before.

What was next? Trial? Conviction? Juvenile detention? It could really go down that way. It was no joke.

His one consolation was that he was sitting here alone, and that Ben was not beside him, about to share his fate. Ditto Pitch, Savannah, Logan, Melissa — even Darren. He could not predict what the future might hold. But he prayed he would have the strength to follow through on his plan to take all the blame.

Detective Sergeant Vizzini was still typing the same page. The man had to be the slowest typist on the planet. Each labored click was a jarring hammerblow to Griffin's raw nerves. *How did I get myself into this?*

"Griffin —" came a voice from behind him.

Dad was a mess — pajama top instead of a shirt, sweatpants, slippers, trench coat, bed hair. He had never looked better, not to Griffin. He ran into his father's arms, blubbering like a two-year-old.

"I'm sorry, Dad! I'm *so* sorry!"

"It's okay, son."

But it *wasn't* okay. It might never be okay.

Vizzini pulled the sheet from the typewriter and placed it on the table in front of Griffin. "Sign here at the bottom."

Griffin backed away from the page like it was a live serpent. A confession? Worse? "What does it say?"

"Take it easy," the officer soothed. "It's just

a statement that you found the baseball card inside the old Rockford house."

Griffin was bewildered. "What do you need that for?"

"There's a lady in Baltimore named Winnifred Rockford-Bates. She's ninety-seven years old, and she's the last surviving member of the original Rockford family. The card is really hers. So it might be some consolation to you that your friend Palomino is out of luck."

"And what happens after I sign?" Griffin quavered.

"Then we go home," Dad said gently.

What? Go home? Was that even possible?

Griffin wheeled to face the sergeant. "Really?"

Vizzini looked stern. "I hope you know how lucky you are. Mr. Palomino isn't going to press charges. He wants to avoid an investigation into whether *he* broke the law when he cheated you. It's a pretty happy ending all around — probably happier than you deserve."

"Thanks, Officer. Thanks a lot!"

As he and his father walked to the car, Griffin took note of a slight bite in the early morning air. A hint of the coming winter — or maybe it was just the smell of freedom. He knew full well how close he had come to losing his.

Mr. Bing pulled onto the road. "Funny the way things work out," he commented. "Even if Palomino hadn't hoodwinked you into selling that card, it still wouldn't be yours. In the end, it would always have belonged to that little old lady in Baltimore."

Griffin nodded, glum despite his relief. "It would have been great, though. A million bucks. Hundreds of thousands, anyway."

His father sighed. "Maybe it's a sign. Money isn't supposed to be easy."

"I don't care about easy money," Griffin mumbled. "I just don't want to have to sell our house and move away."

Mr. Bing jammed on the brakes, and the car screeched to a halt in the middle of the deserted street. "We haven't even had a chance to tell you yet!"

Griffin was alarmed. "Tell me what?"

"All that publicity from the baseball card has generated a storm of interest in the SmartPick! I've got investors who are going to back me through the whole process!"

Griffin stared at his father. "You mean —?"

"We're not selling the house anymore! We're going to be just fine!"

32

N ever thought I'd see *you* again."

Logan Kellerman stepped onto the porch at 530 Park Avenue Extension and stood in front of the elderly man in the rocking chair. "How are you, Mr. Mulroney?" he asked.

"Older and wiser. I now know that your sudden interest in backgammon was to keep me from noticing what was going on across the street. I have to admit it — I never took you for a burglar."

Logan shuffled uncomfortably. "I'm not. I'm an actor."

"Well, you must be a good one," Mulroney

growled. "You sure fooled me. I thought I had a friend."

"It wasn't all acting," Logan admitted. And when he got no reply, he took out the backgammon board and began to set it up on the rickety table between them.

The retired miner eyed him suspiciously. "Don't tell me — Pal-o-mine's got a set of silver candlesticks that you missed on the first go-round."

Logan pulled up a chair. "What's the count — seventeen to fourteen?"

Mulroney snorted. "In your dreams, little man. You never won more than twelve games from me."

Logan threw the dice. "The comeback starts today."

Mrs. Winnifred Rockford-Bates of Baltimore, Maryland, was an eccentric multimillionaire who thought Babe Ruth was a candy bar.

She generously gave her 1920 baseball card to her youngest relative — Darren Vader of Cedarville, New York.

Griffin took it hard. "I always believed that planning was everything. But no plan could ever insulate you from a calamity like this!"

"Darren kept saying he was related to the Rockfords," Ben reminded him. "We didn't think he was telling the truth."

"There's a first time for everything, I guess." Griffin moaned. "This is the end of the world."

It was even less comfort when the card sold for $974,000, making it the second most valuable sports collectible in history.

"He won't get to enjoy one cent of it," Ben predicted in an effort to console his friend. "His folks will make him put it in the bank for college or something."

The reality was even better than that. Darren's parents didn't want their son to reap the benefits of a robbery. They forced him to donate most of the money to the Cedarville

Museum. The large gift put the building fund over the top and allowed construction to begin.

As the bulldozers roared to life on one side of town, on the other, Palomino's Emporium of Collectibles and Memorabilia closed its doors for good. The store had never recovered from the scandal that its owner had cheated Griffin out of the Babe Ruth card. S. Wendell Palomino moved to California, leaving only one thing behind: his dog Luthor, who was sent to the town pound. The Doberman spent less than an hour there before being adopted by Savannah Drysdale. It was a match made in heaven.

The Cedarville Museum opened on schedule the next summer on the site where the old Rockford house had once stood. The townspeople turned out in force for the dedication ceremony, and toured the exhibits of artifacts from pioneer times and memorials to war heroes who had grown up in the area.

What everybody knew, but no one was willing to admit, was that the most interesting thing that had ever happened in this sleepy little community was the Great Baseball Card Heist. That was why the biggest crowd lingered in front of a large framed photograph of seven sixth graders.

The plaque mentioned nothing about the famous robbery. It read:

**SPECIAL THANKS TO
DARREN VADER, LOGAN KELLERMAN,
MELISSA DUKAKIS, ANTONIA
BENSON, SAVANNAH DRYSDALE,
BENJAMIN SLOVAK, AND GRIFFIN BING
FOR A JOB WELL DONE.**

The picture hung opposite a large window overlooking the building's adjoining skate park, which had been a condition of the museum's largest single donation.

The idea for the park came from an old proposal that had been found in the file. Its author was one of the seven in the photograph — the ringleader, The Man With The Plan.